# What People

"Knowing the main c
deeply by this first nove
and understand the trauma of making choices and trusting in God to guide. Anna caught this well when presenting the various decision-making points in choosing a ministry, choosing a mate, where to serve, and how to respond when faced with major and unexpected challenges. BIG decision, *n'est-ce pas*?"

*Arlin Hendrix*
*Missionary in Lyon, France*

"What a great book! I was brought to tears more than once as I read this story of a family's joys and struggles on the mission field. It is a very real portrayal of what life on the mission field can be like, showing all the raw emotions that a missionary might go through. I was truly touched and inspired!"

*Martha Smith*
*Missionary in Mozambique, Africa*

"A first book is probably much like being pregnant. You have all of this inside of you, and it just has to come out. You don't know what it will look like, but it is yours. I was enthralled from the beginning. I read it fast, wanting to find out what happened. I have already started to read it again, more slowly this time. But even at speed, I stopped several times and said prayers of thankfulness for God's provision. I am always touched when our creator stops to answer our prayers of need, and several times in Marcie and Jack's story they asked for and received a sign from God.

"Anna developed the characters well. Jack showed real human tendencies of doubt and self-questioning. I loved that he is human like the rest of us. And I was blown away by Marcie's ability to manage four children in a foreign country and still be active in Bible teaching and encouraging.

"I am looking forward to Anna's next book. This one ends too soon. I want to follow Jack and Marcie a while longer and see how those four kids turn out. Kudos to the author, mother of three, pastor's wife, schoolteacher, and Bible study instructor."

*Liz Adams*
*Retired medical technologist in Perry, Georgia*

"If you think you are too ordinary to be used by God, then you need to read this story. It is a beautifully constructed narrative about the joys and struggles of a young family on the mission field. I highly recommend it to you, especially if you're considering a life of vocational ministry."

*Barrett Coffman*
*Pulpit Minister at Southside Church of Christ in Lexington,*
*Kentucky*

# JACK'S JOURNEY

## ORDINARY MAN. EXTRAORDINARY MISSION.

**Anna Caulley**

To: Betty

God bless you!

Ann M. Caulley

Hebrews 12: 1

Editorial services by Karen Roberts, RQuest, LLC.

This book is biographical fiction and is based in part on stories from the lives of missionaries who served overseas in the 1970s and 1980s.

For questions or to request a speaking engagement, contact the author at annacaulley@hotmail.com.

ISBN-13: 978-1515314905
ISBN-10: 1515314901

Printed in the United States of America

# DEDICATION

For Dad and Mom, Buddy and Maurine Jones. Thank you for your godly examples.

# CONTENTS

# FOREWORD

It turns out our daughter was paying attention more than we thought as my wife and I occasionally told stories about how our "romance" began. Over the past few years, she has asked us for more details about many things that happened in our years in St. Louis, Missouri, and then in Geneva, Switzerland, and in Nantes, France. Maurine and I have enjoyed reliving the memories and discussing them with her. Little did we know she was writing a book based on our story.

We are deeply honored that Anna wanted to create this story based in part on our lives, and she has done a fantastic job as a writer, as you will see in reading her work. But this book is fiction, biographical fiction. Some of the incidents are surprisingly true to actuality, but certainly not all of them. This work, her first novel, brings tears of joy to our eyes as we remember the early days of our life together. Anna has taken some real events, added doses of fiction, and created excitement and drama, which make an inspiring story. The overall message, that God uses ordinary people and makes their lives extraordinary, is true.

There are two important differences from the reality of our lives as missionaries overseas that I want to note for the reader, who may not know the true story. First, the interpersonal conflict moments depicted in the book are not based on real events or real people. We were blessed to work with some of the greatest people in the world, and some of their strengths and contributions to our lives are portrayed by characters in the book. There were failings and sad times to be sure, but Anna wisely did not want to implicate other real people by describing those times. Anna added some "spice" and some sadness, which can happen in and around everyone's life and certainly in the life and work of all missionaries. The worst crises in the book did not happen in reality in our work.

It is important to note here that the other characters in this story are more dreamed up than memories of actual people. For those readers who know the other people involved with us in the work, you might wonder if some of the bad things in the book actually happened in their lives. Please assume they did not. If you want to know about the real characters we met and worked with in those years, ask us. We would love to hear from you and share our stories.

Anna has generously portrayed her dad as a missionary leader and hero. I am deeply touched. However, those who were there know that for the first ten years in Geneva and Nantes, the man I was blessed to work with was more the leader of the team, even though we did work as equal partners. The souls brought to Christ, the excitement of seeing hundreds of people come to public meetings and scores of them continue to meet with us, the amazing joy of watching a new church begin—none of it would have happened without the leadership of Bob Grigg and his wife, Patti, and their children, Brandon and Stephanie. We are forever indebted to them for their friendship, their deep spirituality, and their evangelistic zeal. They are not the coworkers depicted in this book. Also, so many others who were great friends and coworkers are not included in the story, nor are events that transpired in the last three years of our time in France with these coworkers. Anna is not attempting to tell any of their stories. She is taking parts of her mom and dad's story and creating the rest.

Now that you know some background information, sit back and enjoy the book. Laugh, cry, and blush in embarrassment for the characters as you imagine yourself in their situation. Thrill to see how the God of heaven brings people to Himself through anything and everything His people do in an effort to serve Him. Let yourself be inspired to see what the Lord Jesus can do with even the simplest, most ordinary people—and someone like you.

Thank you, Anna. You must have gotten your writing talent from your mother.

Buddy Jones, proud father
Columbus, Georgia
July 2015

# PREFACE

I have a story to tell. It is about what being a missionary is really like. I do not wish to write a Hollywood missionary story, nor do I wish to paint a false, unrealistic, overly Christian picture. My story is about missionaries who do not have movies made about them: the non-famous ones. The ones that don't necessarily go to third-world countries.

What is missionary life for them like, day in and day out? What happens when missionaries follow God's call and then find themselves in a desert place of the soul? Why do things not always go "according to plan" when they are doing what they think is God's will?

This novel, a work of fiction, is based on stories from the lives of missionaries in the 1970s and 1980s. My goal in writing it is to show that God uses ordinary people who commit themselves to Him to do extraordinary things. He takes the mundane and transforms it into the marvelous, showing us His power. He takes regular people and makes them famous in His name. He gets in the muck and mire with us and pulls out that "diamond in the rough."

My message is simple: God can use *you* no matter how ordinary your life is. Whether you are a sales rep, a migrant worker, a deejay for the local radio station, a fitness instructor, a landscape business owner, or a stay-at-home mom, He wants you to open your eyes and see that others are waiting to receive a message from you, and some have a message from God *for* you.

*Jack's Journey* is in part my parents' story, but it is also my own story and that of ministers and missionaries I know. Having experienced the ministry side of mission work both as a child and as an adult, I know what it is like to feel a strong call from the Lord and then to be thrown into mediocrity and failure. Life's circumstances can chip away at dreams and cause doubts in God and in self. Persevering through miles of suffering and even silence from God leads to victory. God brings beauty even from the ashes of defeat.

What really happens between the calling of the Lord and the fulfillment of a prophecy? What are the options when one misses the boat and heads down the wrong path that seemed so right at first?

Can God redeem humanness, error, and wrongdoing? These are the questions that I wrestle with in *Jack's Journey*.

In these pages, you will not find the martyrdom of some who have gone to the bush of Papua New Guinea, nor will you find a prosperity gospel promising happily-ever-after if you follow God's call. This book is about experiencing the not-so-romantic and not-so-perilous side of mission work and persevering. It is a true picture of mission work, not a perfect one.

# ACKNOWLEDGMENTS

You would not be holding this book in your hands if it wasn't for my husband, Don. He saw the potential in me and in this work long before I did. He kept me going on the project when I felt like quitting. He allowed me to leave our three sons with him at home over and over again so that I could find a quiet place of inspiration. Thank you, Don, for tirelessly listening to me read hundreds of excerpts and for giving me honest feedback. A special thanks goes to my three boys for being patient while I spent hours reading, revising, and typing.

Mom and Dad, thanks to you, I had a story to tell. Some people *go* on adventures, while I was privileged to *live* an adventure. I thank both of you for giving me permission to steal from your lives and for allowing me to take liberties with certain parts of your story to create this work of fiction.

Thank you, Karen Roberts, my editor, for being my coach, for encouraging me to persevere, and for not giving up on me. Thank you for going above and beyond the call of duty by sending me inspiring articles and helpful suggestions along the way on top of your regular edits to polish the manuscript. I also thank my aunt and proofreader, Peggy Carter, who pointed me in the right direction at the very beginning of this project and steered me toward success.

My heartfelt thanks goes to several others who helped this book become a reality. I thank Caroline Crownover for being a fan of my writing, for having favorite passages, and for encouraging me with constructive criticism. Melanie Jones, thank you for reading my original manuscript and helping me think through specific passages. Mike Mason, thank you for giving me very useful feedback on grammatical structure. Thank you, Eryn Jones, for reading my original manuscript and for offering positive feedback. Thanks also to my brother, Daniel Jones, and my longtime friend and missionary, Martha Smith, for offering some extra help with editing details.

A very special thanks goes to the following individuals who sponsored me financially during this project and who believed that I could bring it to completion: Linda Davis, Nancy McClendon, Uncle Ralph McCluggage, Anna Dreyfus, Mom and Dad (Buddy and Maurine Jones), Sarah Greer, and Mike Caulley Sr.

Most of all, I give thanks to God, my Lord and Savior. My wish is to glorify Him through this book.

# PART I

# Hearing the Call

# CHAPTER 1

Jack Jones held his head in his hands, his strong fingers buried in his disheveled, chocolate-brown hair. He pressed his lips firmly together in an effort to withhold emotion because after all, guys don't cry. Especially grown men, who should have their lives together and be sailing toward the future with great confidence.

Sitting on a concrete bench, he glanced at his reflection in the campus fountain pool, lit up by a few blinking lights at its center.

"Jack!" a voice yelled out from behind him. "Boy, did you ever miss out! Every single JuGoJu girl was there. Even you could have had a date tonight."

Jack straightened and looked up at his good friend Jay Spencer with a weak smile. "No kidding?" he said, trying to sound cheerful. JuGoJu was a popular girls' club on campus.

"I'm serious! The auditorium was packed out for movie night, and my date was really groovy. You missed a great opportunity, buddy!" As if sensing Jack's mood, he tampered down his enthusiasm. "What have you been doing all night? Did you see Marcie?"

"I . . . I talked to her . . . this afternoon. If you must know, she says . . . she says she's not ready for a relationship with me."

Frowning, Jay remained silent for a few seconds. "Oh, dumped you like she did Gary, huh?" he said at last.

Jack looked down. "I guess so. Truth is, stepping out on faith sounded a lot easier on Sunday, sitting in church, than it did today." Lifting his head, he stared at his reflection in the fountain pool on the Harding University campus. The lights inside the pool took turns blinking on and off, casting their low light into the near darkness of the evening.

Jay sat down beside him. "I'm sorry, man."

"I gave up a degree in engineering to become a missionary to France," Jack burst out. "Some of my professors thought it was a stupid move, but I genuinely felt God's leading. Now I'm beginning to wonder about that too."

"Well, you look like a Frenchie to me!" Jay said, grinning. "Have you heard anything yet about your application to that missionary training program in St. Louis?"

"You know, I was supposed to get a letter by May first letting me know whether I'd been accepted. But I haven't heard a word. I guess that means all the interns have been chosen by now. Another door slammed in my face."

Jack leaned back against the bench, hands behind his head, his lean, six-foot frame stretched out. His piercing brown eyes and defined nose almost gave him the look of a sophisticated Frenchman, but his usual broad smile was enough to wipe away any trace of cosmopolitan flare. His looks and friendly personality had won him the senior class president's office that year.

"I'm a senior, Jay! I'm twenty-two years old. I'm supposed to have my life together. What am I going to do with a Bible major if I don't become a missionary? Oh, and then there's the wife thing. Don't get me started on Marcie again," he added in a mutter.

Jay remained silent and looked down.

*God, can you just send me a sign? Did I misread you?* The silence was heavy. It seemed to suck in Jack's prayer as soon as he'd thought it. His shoulders drooped. The evening had turned cool. Clouds were moving in and the wind had picked up. He glanced across the well manicured, two-hundred-acre Arkansas campus and sighed heavily. "I guess I'd better come up with plan B."

"Grad school?" Jay suggested.

Jack gave a short laugh. "Applications were due long ago."

"Find a job here in Searcy and apply again next semester?"

"No way. Maybe I should just go back home to Greenville." Jack's expression looked as glum as he felt.

"Hey, you're a Texan, born and bred!" Jay said heartily, elbowing Jack in the ribs. "A little setback isn't going to keep you down for long."

Jack forced a smile. "I could work with my dad at the local radio station. He's always wanted that." His stomach lurched at the thought.

"Look, Jack, if God wants you to be a missionary, He will show you the way for it to happen. It just might not be at the time you choose. But if He promised it, He will bring it about."

Jack sat up straighter, the truth of his friend's words resounding in his heart. "You're right," he said with a certain amount of hope, albeit small. "I committed to be faithful, and that includes when things aren't going the way I expected. I'll keep

4

asking for God's leading, and I'll walk through whatever door He opens up. Even if it feels like a detour—or a dead end." He took a deep breath and let it out. "God can use even that for His glory."

---

Marcie Lewis ran by the front desk in the lobby of Cathcart Dormitory and then past the dorm mom's quarters. As soon as she turned left to dash for room 124, her roommate, Nancy Moore, motioned to her from the other end of the hallway with a frantic finger over her lips. Putting both hands out in front of her and opening her fingers wide, Nancy displayed a stop-right-where-you-are motion. Marcie's heart sank.

Nancy and Marcie shared a suite with Sarah Gray, the dorm's resident assistant, who was sitting inside room 123 with the door ajar. Sarah was not the type to make friends. She was a full-blooded nerd: slightly overweight, glasses, never wore make-up, rarely combed her hair, and made no bones about sharing her extensive mathematical knowledge. She took her campus job all too seriously: she held every dorm resident to the minute of the ten o'clock curfew. It was impossible to fool her. She could somehow catch the sneakiest, late-night sprinter the minute she was late getting back to her room.

This particular weekend, Sarah had gone out of town and wasn't expected back until Sunday afternoon. But she had apparently decided to return one day early, much to Marcie's dismay. She had already accrued twenty-two late minutes so far this term. If Sarah caught her tonight, she would exceed her limit of late minutes allotted for one semester, which would mean she would be "dormed" for the rest of the weekend. Of this fate, there was only one potential escape: Marcie would have to sneak past room 123 and into Nancy's room without Sarah seeing her.

"Marcie, is that you?" a voice called out from inside 123. Sarah's direct question threw cold water on Marcie's high hopes.

"Hey, Sarah," Marcie muttered, defeated.

"Got your card?"

"Oh, um, okay."

Marcie walked sheepishly back toward the front desk to retrieve her late-minutes card and bring it to Sarah, who seemed to take excessive pleasure in recording the seventeen extra minutes.

"I guess this means you will be inside for the rest of the weekend," Sarah announced, a bit too cheerfully for Marcie.

Instead of commenting, Marcie put her card back in its place, feigned apathy as she sauntered to her room, and then clicked the door shut with a little extra oomph. *Now what?*

Ordinarily Marcie would have snapped something back at Sarah, but on this night she felt relieved to be dormed. She finally had the excuse she needed to be alone for a while. She had already seen the evening's slated campus movie, *Butch Cassidy and the Sundance Kid*. Her date, some Walter guy, had bored her even more than the film.

The flop of a date wasn't the most nagging thought on Marcie's mind though. She kept torturing herself by replaying part of a conversation she'd had with Jack earlier that day at Harding Park.

"Marcie, would you like to enter into a dating relationship with me?"

"I'm sorry, Jack. I'm not ready for that yet. It's still too soon after . . . "

"I understand," Jack said, stopping her short.

*Why did he have to be so awkward about asking me to be his girlfriend?* Yet even as she reflected back on their conversation, she regretted turning him down so quickly.

Nancy jolted Marcie's thoughts back to the present. "So, is Walter everything you thought he was going to be? Isn't he dreamy?" Her voice oozed with curiosity, and her eyes searched Marcie's face.

*Walter? Who cared about him?* Torn with thoughts of Gary and Jack, Marcie barely had energy left to think about her escort to the campus movie tonight. She answered coldly. "Who gives a care? I don't see why everybody's so worked up over him. He's just like Gary. They're all the same."

Nancy knew Marcie's mention of Gary meant that Walter might as well close the coffin on his hopes of ever seeing Marcie again. Gary had broken her heart, and Marcie had decided to let him go. Six months had passed since the break up, and Nancy wondered if Marcie would ever get over him. In order to help Marcie move on to more exciting horizons, she was constantly setting Marcie up on

6

blind dates, to no avail. Tonight was no different. Marcie's knight in shining armor remained hidden.

Marcie and Nancy's senior year was practically over now, and Nancy was finally ready to give up her quest to help her roommate find her one true love. She had hoped Marcie might return from her latest date at least somewhat happier than usual because of what she was about to reveal. Losing all patience, she exploded with her big news.

"I'm engaged! And I want you to be the maid of honor!"

As soon as the words left her mouth, she longed to retrieve them. But Marcie left her no time to apologize.

"Nancy, that's wonderful! Of course, I would love to be your maid of honor! When did it happen? Tell me everything!"

Nancy fumbled the details. Her excitement was dampened by her desire to see her best friend happy too.

"Look, Nancy, I know you're worried about me. Don't be. I've decided I'm going to be single. It's going to be fine! Just think of all the options I'll have being unattached."

Nancy shrugged sadly. It seemed inevitable. Marcie was going to make it through the so-called marriage factory of a Christian college unhitched!

---

Late into the night, long after Nancy had fallen asleep, Marcie buried her face in her pillow, pleading with God to make her as brave as she had pretended to be when she heard Nancy's news. Unexpectedly her thoughts turned to Jack. She remembered his exact words, asking her to "enter into a dating relationship." *Who would say such a thing these days? Had his dad coached him on how to talk to girls?* she wondered as a smile crept onto her face. Yet Jack's question was noble and sincere, and she knew it. She cringed slightly at the memory of his hurt face. Had she been too harsh? She couldn't bear the thought.

Well, it wouldn't do her any good to stew about it. What was done was done. She would show the world that she could do just fine by herself. She would graduate, get a teaching job, and who knows, maybe even someday do mission work. God would use her in powerful ways. She knew it. She just had to be brave.

# CHAPTER 2

It was a crisp, autumn afternoon in West Memphis, a sprawling Arkansas metropolis with a plethora of opportunities for young career women in the 1970s. Bordered on one side by the Mississippi River, the city boasted a rich history of European explorers and Civil War battles. Marcie Lewis, 1972 Harding University graduate, had moved to West Memphis to pursue a career as a teacher. She enjoyed her weekday afternoon walks from school to the trailer house where she lived with two other women, Nancy and Judy, both also Harding University alums.

Marcie was in her second year of teaching fourth grade at West Memphis Christian School. Most of the time, she stayed very busy in the big city with writing lesson plans, tutoring, attending little league games, volunteering at church, and attending singles' events. She was thankful to have little to no down time. Although she had bravely stated to Nancy on that infamous night of her senior year at Harding that she would remain single, she couldn't help but feel haunted by lonely feelings when she had long, quiet moments to herself. She had begun to allow herself to hope that she might meet someone here in West Memphis.

This past summer, after Nancy's engagement had fallen through, she gladly accepted Marcie's invitation to share rent on a trailer with her and another former JuGoJu sister, Judy. Marcie and Nancy were both teachers, and Judy was a receptionist at a dentist's office. Most of the time the modest trailer family room was littered with lesson plans, grade books, and craft cutouts. The three of them took turns cleaning and cooking for each other, and they loved to entertain coworkers and church friends.

As Marcie continued her walk home from school, she mentally recapped her day. It was Friday and the children had been restless, awaiting the arrival of the Thanksgiving holidays next week. The classroom was anything but peaceful. Marcie sighed. She needed the upcoming break as much as the kids did.

She felt pretty in her straight, green, polyester dress—her favorite teacher dress because of the pattern of little green apples. It felt warm against her skin as she moved her legs easily, gracefully in the afternoon sun. She glanced at her slim profile in the afternoon shadow. Her light brown hair tumbled softly over her shoulders as her bright blue eyes fell to the ground, mechanically searching for crisp leaves that would crunch pleasingly beneath her feet.

She was pretty in a natural way and didn't require much make-up to bring out her already attractive features: a ready smile on her lips, straight teeth, high cheekbones, and big, blue eyes.

*Twenty-three years old and still unmarried,* she mused. A prayer formed from somewhere deep inside of her. "Dear God, I have been out of college for over a year now. I haven't had a single date, and I'm not interested in anyone here. I know if You wanted to, You could drop someone down out of the sky. Please help my unbelief!"

Her brisk walking came to an abrupt halt. She stared blankly ahead at the passing cars and changing streetlights. In her daze, she'd missed her heavenly Father's hand at work in the beautiful sunset and the evening concert of the robin red breasts in the trees above. Nature's wonders were overshadowed by a first-time thought: she, Marcie Lewis, truly might never marry.

Stepping into the trailer, Marcie was pulled out of her thoughts by Nancy's friendly greeting. "Marcie, it's the week-end! Then two more school days until Thanksgiving break!"

"Yeah, groovy," Marcie said sarcastically.

"Come on, let's have dinner. Judy cooked poppy seed chicken."

The three women grabbed plates of food and plopped down on the sofa. Marcie picked at her food and made lousy company. As usual, Nancy tried to cheer her up.

"Marcie, just think. You'll have the holiday to rest up. Then you'll have extra energy for the Christmas season."

The thought of handling the children amidst more chaos was altogether too much for Marcie, and she was relieved when Nancy and Judy went on to discuss their plans for Thanksgiving.

"So, where are you going, Marcie?" Nancy asked when they had finished.

"Well, I don't know yet. I'll figure something out."

"You're welcome to come home with me," Nancy said. Judy quickly chimed in with an invitation to her house as well.

"It's all right. I need to spend some time at home with my parents, I guess."

But somehow going home didn't feel right this year. Marcie wanted to get away, to get off on her own and do something different. Nancy sensed her reluctance.

"Hey, Marcie, why don't you just get over yourself and go see Jack in St. Louis?" Nancy asked.

"Are you crazy?" Marcie retorted, surprised at her friend's insight. "Are you suggesting that I throw myself at him? I'm not that kind of girl. And I'm not even interested."

———————

November 19, 1973, was an unseasonably warm day in St. Louis. Jack Jones pulled his car up to Cutting Edge Photofinishers at four o'clock after finishing his last sales call of the day. He shared an office with three other reps, two of whom smoked at least one pack of cigarettes a day. If he didn't have a good work ethic, the fumes from the office would be enough motivation to stay in the field all day doing something, anything, to avoid the office. Today, however, he was back an hour before quitting time. He had just delivered some advertising posters to the new grocery store on the west side of town. Tired from a busy Monday, he was returning a bit earlier than normal to his smoke-infested office. The world of film developing was thriving. Businesses like his seemed to attract new customers without much effort. The product, photos, sold itself, so his work was both profitable and plentiful.

In the evenings and three afternoons each week, Jack pursued an entirely different line of work—the career he'd almost given up over a year ago. He was working as an intern at McAlister Road Church of Christ and training to be a missionary to France. The morning after his prayer of desperation by the fountain pool at Harding, he'd received that phone call he'd been waiting for, offering him the coveted internship. His dream was coming true after all.

*God's timing has proved impeccable*, he mused.

He parked his 1961 Ford Falcon, which he had inherited from his father, in the office lot skillfully. He was proud of the eleven-year-old vehicle. During his time at Harding, he had only driven it to and from college, so it was still in fairly good condition. The engine was small and not very powerful, but it was his, and he was thankful to have it at his disposal. He remembered the day he'd

10

received it from his father. It had only 30,000 miles on it. He looked at the odometer, which currently read 56,000 miles. He felt a bond with the vehicle after four plus years of owning it.

Jack climbed up the office stairs, holding his briefcase in one hand and an empty McDonald's bag of trash in the other. He entered the smoky office, trying not to breathe too deeply. He tossed his briefcase on his desk and his lunch remains in the trashcan. Just as he reached for his daily paperwork, the phone on his desk rang. He waited until the second ring to pick up. Maybe it would be the last phone call of the day he would have to answer.

"Cutting Edge. This is Jack," he said evenly.

"Hi, Jack. I was just calling to see if we are still on for tonight."

The syrupy voice from the other end was that of Casey Wright. He'd asked her to get a cola with him before church tonight. He was only partially looking forward to the rendezvous.

Casey was cute enough. She was fairly short and had a thin figure. Her blonde, curly hair bobbed up and down when she walked. She had fair skin, brown eyes, and a nose that was a little bit small and pinched but not overly so. Her chin was very square, but her curly hair softened the edge of her face. It reached just to her shoulders, and its curliness stole everyone's gaze away from her facial outline. She was very much into fashion and was always careful to choose clothing that brought out the best features in her face and figure. But it was Casey's personality that won people over: she was bubbly and cheerful all the time. Nobody had ever known Casey Wright to have a bad day.

Though she was a couple of years younger than Jack, Casey was obviously smitten with him. For his part, Jack liked her pretty well. Truthfully, he had not shown serious interest in any girl since Marcie Lewis during his senior year at Harding. Now, a year and a half later, he figured it was time for him to give dating a shot again. Casey attended all of the church meetings, came from a strong Christian family, and seemed very interested in mission work. He couldn't find a reason not to ask her out, so he finally did.

Since moving to St. Louis and starting his internship, Jack had been consumed with ministry. He'd found fulfillment in leading devotionals on Mondays, heading up prayer meetings, participating in Bible studies, and visiting folks in the hospital. There was little

11

time to have much of a personal life; nevertheless, he still hoped getting married was an option for him. *Why not go ahead and try to find some possibilities? Casey seems to be a readily available one,* he reasoned.

He responded to Casey's phone call with a confident voice, careful not to show too much excitement about a first date. "You bet. I'll pick you up at 5."

"Great! I'll be ready!"

Casey was always super enthusiastic. Jack told himself that perhaps it was just her way of giving him the encouragement he needed to ask her out. Surely she was not really that excited all the time.

He finished his day's paperwork, picked up his briefcase, and headed back to the parking lot. The Falcon started successfully. It was becoming a gamble as to whether or not the old car would start on the first try. It didn't have air conditioning, so the fall weather was an immense relief for his home commute compared to the typically sultry summer days of St. Louis. As he pulled out of the lot, he saw that traffic was bumper-to-bumper, as it was every weekday from three to five, but he'd learned to deal with it. Though his office was downtown, the hours were nonnegotiable, and when traffic was slow, he used the time to think. Today he started out thinking about what he would share that evening at church and then slipped into his habit of dreaming about changing the world.

He loved the work at McAlister Road Church. He intended to duplicate what he was learning there and take it overseas. He could still hear his favorite Bible professor's words: "The number of Christian churches in the United States of America far outweighs those in other places in the world." Jack knew in that moment that he wanted to help bring balance to the world.

During his junior year at Harding, he had participated in a campaign to the international city of Geneva, Switzerland. There he saw scores of foreigners come to know the Lord. He caught a vision for Europe as being a great balancing point, a place where people from different nationalities converged, where foreigners could be reached. He had great hope that they would return to their places of origin, in turn share their faith, and start new churches. It was a grand vision. Nothing was impossible with God.

In the Church of Christ, missionaries were required to raise all of their own support as well as make important decisions such as how long to stay in the target city. Unlike some churches, the one he belonged to didn't send missionaries with a set "term of service" in mind. And there was no definite assignment as far as location. All of the financial responsibility and major decision making were up to those who believed to be called by God into missions. As he imagined his future, Jack wondered how long he would be willing to live in a foreign country. Would it be short? Would it be for life?

He was experiencing much success in leadership at McAlister Road Church. The singles' group had grown from twenty-five to one hundred. If a group of Christian singles in St. Louis, Missouri, could experience that much growth in such a short time, what changes and growth could happen through the efforts of a dedicated team of missionaries in a lifetime? He could see it now: they would begin in France—church plants in Paris, and then in Lyon or Marseilles? Within a five-year time frame, churches could be planted in all the major French cities. After five more years, each beginning church could send church planters across the borders to Spain, Luxembourg, Belgium, Switzerland, Germany, Italy, and beyond. How simple it was in his mind: all of Europe could be evangelized during his lifetime. *That* fired him up.

Suddenly he realized that he was in Casey's neighborhood. As he pulled up to her house, he said a brief prayer, asking God to bless the singles' meeting tonight.

———————————

Casey had been watching from the front window of her house, counting down the hours and then minutes until the time of Jack's arrival to take her out. Jack was her dream boy. She loved how mature he was and how everyone at church respected him. She thought he was the cutest, and he was smart too. Secretly she thought that she didn't deserve anyone quite like Jack. When he asked her to go with him to the meeting and get a soda tonight, she thought she had died and gone to heaven. She could hardly contain her excitement and only hoped that she wouldn't say anything too foolish during their date and ruin any chance that she might have to be his girlfriend—something she tried to forbid herself from thinking about for fear that it might not come true and then her hopes would be ruined.

To her, a date with Jack Jones was almost too good to be true. She had spent the better part of the afternoon preparing for the evening. She had fixed her hair four different ways before settling on the flipped out look; she had bought a new pair of earrings and had ironed six outfits only to pick out one that didn't need it. Even with all of the preparations she had made, she felt she would never be as ready as she wanted to be. She wanted to be perfect.

When she saw the famous Ford Falcon turn the corner into her driveway at last, she ran to the door and then forced herself to wait a little longer before answering the doorbell so as not to appear too eager.

Jack couldn't help but notice her flattering, knee-length tan skirt and green sweater and her blond hair bobbing up and down as she bee-bopped down the sidewalk with him to his car. *She looks very pretty tonight,* he thought as he opened the door for her. For the most part, he liked her butterfly personality, which could sometimes be a little overwhelming. At least she was easy to talk to. For this, Jack was very grateful. He didn't like feeling the pressure of keeping a conversation going, especially on a date.

They quickly settled on Steak 'n Shake as their destination, just a few blocks away. Without a wait, they were seated in a booth, where the waitress brought them orange freezes. Casey talked about her day, what happened at Savvy Salon, where she worked as a hairdresser while still taking college courses for a speech pathology degree. Jack talked about his day's work as well. The conversation flowed freely, but it had to be cut short by the time. Jack certainly couldn't be late for church.

Thirty minutes later, the two of them entered the church auditorium and sat down together in the second row for the Monday night meeting. Jack felt several pairs of eyes noticing the fact that he had walked in with Casey and was now sitting with her. During the second singing of "The Steadfast Love of the Lord," Jack noticed the smile on Casey's face. He also noticed her arm resting on the back of his chair. He tried to tell himself it was a good sign. Presently, however, it was his turn to share his thoughts, and he had no time to think about her advances. He rose and walked to the front of the group.

14

"Tonight," Jack began, "I want to talk to you about sharing your faith and not being ashamed of the gospel. Sharing the gospel is a risk that we have to take. God commands us to do it. It costs some people their lives, as it did for Stephen, who was stoned to death in Acts 7. But Phillip, who shared his faith with the Ethiopian eunuch, did not die for sharing his faith. Why, you might ask, do some have to die for the faith and others don't? If this question is on your mind, you are asking the wrong question. Instead, you should ask, 'Lord, what do you want me to do? Where am I to go?' When He answers, your reply should be the same as Isaiah's, which was, 'Here am I, send me.'"

"Amen!" several shouted out. The excitement in the room was palpable. Three people decided to give their lives to Jesus that very night, which meant that the group moved to the main sanctuary where the baptistery was. In the Churches of Christ, baptism happened immediately. *This is what being a Christian is all about,* Jack thought to himself.

He wanted to stay at church longer and fellowship with the new believers in the group, so he was disappointed to have to leave the group earlier than usual to take Casey home. It felt more burdensome than he expected.

When he finally shifted mental gears, he found Casey to be pleasant company once again. As he drove her home, he kept telling himself to give her more of a chance. Even so, he struggled to pry himself away from where his heart was. If he could, he would throw himself completely into his work at church. His ministry was the only thing that truly gave him pleasure. *It's not the same as being a workaholic,* he reasoned, *if the work is God's work.*

"Wow," Casey exclaimed as he drove, "that was really something! Jack, you're amazing. I loved your lesson."

Jack felt a little embarrassed. As Casey continued, he felt more and more uncomfortable.

"I'm so excited about the baptisms tonight! You must feel so happy!"

"I do, Casey, but it's nothing that I did."

"But it's just so wonderful! And all those people that came. There must have been a hundred and fifty there tonight!"

Casey chattered on about different church members and then more about her day at work. Finally, after asking for Jack's thoughts

15

about the evening service, she asked if he had any Thanksgiving plans.

"Oh, I am staying in town this year," he answered.

"Jack, please come and eat Thanksgiving dinner with my family this year. We always eat together on Wednesday, the day before, because of everyone's work schedules. Please, will you come?" she begged.

He was reluctant, but didn't see a way out. "That would be great. Thanks for inviting me."

Casey beamed.

*She is a pleasant sort of person,* he thought to himself. He liked her desire to be active in church, and he realized she was the kind of woman he should be pursuing for more than just a casual date. As he pulled into her driveway, he noticed she seemed reluctant to get out of the car.

"Thanks for the orange freeze tonight. It was delicious. I had a great time."

She kept finding some other detail of the evening to talk about. He could tell she didn't want to leave him. It had been a while since he'd thought about anyone as a potential girlfriend. He wondered what it would feel like to kiss Casey. Suddenly, as if overtaken by some unknown force, he decided to try.

Casey melted under his tentative embrace. When he realized she was hoping for more than just a peck good-bye, alarms started flaring all shades of red in his head. He tried his best to pull back, but to his growing shock, he found it took all of his concentration to separate himself from her and to restore her to the passenger seat of the Falcon beside him. He felt himself breaking into a sweat as he opened her car door and walked her up the path to her house.

"Good night, Casey," he said as calmly as he could. She gave him a little wink before closing the door.

*Yikes,* he thought. *Where did that come from?* And to think that he had agreed to see her again in a few days! It was obvious she was head over heels for him. As he drove to his apartment, the feeling of having made a mistake settled down on him heavily. *I should not have asked her out, much less kissed her!*

Traffic was much better on his way home. Jack's roommate, Don, was reading a book when he walked into the apartment.

"There's a message for you," Don said.

"Oh yeah?"

"Yeah, a Marcie called for you, says she's an old college friend. She said to call her back. She'll be up late."

Jack felt something jump inside of him. Marcie? *What in the world could she be calling me about?* The last time he'd seen her was at Harding's homecoming last year. She was civil enough but not warm and certainly far from flirtatious. When he invited her to come and see what the ministry was like in St. Louis, she'd quickly found a reason not to come. Clearly she had many other interests. *What reason could she possibly have for calling me tonight? And with the direction to call her back?*

He quickly dialed the number, which oddly he had somehow memorized.

"Hello, Marcie. It's Jack. Is everything okay?"

"Oh, yes, everything's fine. Sorry to bother you. I, um, I know it's late notice, but I don't have any plans for Thanksgiving this year, and, well, you invited me to come up to see the ministry in St. Louis. I remember you saying the invitation is always open. So, uh, I guess I'm a little embarrassed to ask you, but would it be okay if I took you up on your invitation? I would really like to see what the church work is like there. You make it sound so interesting. Maybe I could come up tomorrow? If you have too much going on, I understand. I know it's really late notice."

Marcie stopped herself from rambling on. Her face felt hot, and she could hardly believe what she was doing. *Of course he would have other plans!*

Jack's voice sounded strong and resolved on the other end. "Marcie, I would love for you to come. When can you get here?"

Relief washed over Marcie as she collected herself enough to make definite plans with Jack about her arrival on Tuesday.

*Ha!* Jack thought as he hung up the phone. *Of all things! Naturally she would decide to come on a weekend when I already have a date*. He thought of Casey. Whatever had jumped inside of him when he heard Marcie's name now settled like a lump into the pit of his stomach as he remembered his promise to eat an early Thanksgiving dinner with Casey's family. *How will I explain to her that I can't fulfill my commitment to be with her and her family for dinner on Wednesday?*

He reminded himself that there had never been anything more than friendship between Marcie and him. Even when they had spent so much time together his senior year—Marcie's campaigning with him when he ran for class president, his helping her learn her lines for the *Doll's House* play, and attending the Homecoming game together—they had only been good friends.

His befuddlement frustrated him. *It's no use. I'll never be anything more to her,* he told himself and grew depressed at the thought. Maybe he would keep his date with Casey on Wednesday, call Marcie back, and tell her she would have to wait until Thursday morning because of an earlier commitment. That would show her clearly where they stood. He didn't want her to feel any sort of obligation toward him, and so he shouldn't feel obligated to her either.

Even as the thought crossed his mind, he knew he couldn't go through with such a plan. He would think it through and figure something out. It was a busy week already. He had a Bible study lined up on Wednesday morning that he felt he could not cancel. And where would she stay? Certainly not with him. He was not the type to host a woman in his apartment overnight. It might raise suspicions, and he wanted to make her as comfortable as possible. The female interns stayed at the "girls' house," a large home downtown that several women from church rented together. He wondered if Marcie would feel comfortable in such a setting. He would call his friend Kelly tomorrow and ask her what she thought.

It took a while for him to fall asleep that night. He read some but felt unusually bored with the words. Eventually, exhaustion took over, and his mind ceased tormenting him with wishful thinking. He had a lot to do in two days. Most important: give his regrets to Casey.

# CHAPTER 3

Marcie sped along newly constructed highway 55 at 54 miles per hour with Simon and Garfunkel singing on the radio. President Carter had mandated that all interstate highway speed limits in the country be lowered to 55 that year. Though nonsensical, it was a law that Marcie would certainly not break. Her dad had always told her that she must not speed. He could forgive fender benders, depending on the circumstances, but speeding was inexcusable. She had told Jack that she would arrive in time for dinner, and she was right on schedule.

She had no idea what to expect from her Thanksgiving holiday. Although she had satisfied Nancy and Judy, who wanted her to do something different and exciting, she was outside of her comfort zone. She considered Jack to be a good friend. But calling him on the phone had made her feel differently. She felt as if she were "making a move" on him. Would he get the wrong idea about their relationship again, as he had back in their senior year at Harding? She was beginning to regret having taken the chance. She tried to distract herself by focusing on her lesson plans for the following week—to no avail.

The sun was shining, and it was unusually warm for late November. The drive was a pleasant one. Although she was not fond of driving long distances, it was a relief to be away from school pressures. She made it as far as Cape Girardeau and stopped for French fries and ketchup—her favorite snack.

Evening had fallen by the time she exited the highway, and within minutes, she was in Jack's neck of the woods. At the stoplight, she checked herself in the mirror, rubbing her cheeks slightly and running her fingers through her hair. She had managed to stay decently put together on the road. Her lips needed color, though.

She pulled into a parking space and thumbed through her purse in search of her tube of lipstick. Holding the cap in one hand and the lipstick in the other, she stopped herself short. *Why am I taking the time to primp? Who am I trying to impress?* She rubbed the pink hue on her lips anyway.

---

Jack was impatient in spite of himself. Casey had reacted well enough to his sheepish regrets, and he had spent most of the day studying for the class that he was supposed to teach on Sunday. He wanted to take full advantage of Marcie's visit. He was trying not to admit to himself that Casey didn't hold a candle to Marcie. Not in personality, intelligence, compatibility with him, or beauty—both inside and out. Marcie's eyes were the purest blue. She always had a fresh look about her. It didn't seem to matter what she wore. Her clothes flattered her attractive figure without being immodest. She had a ready smile. Her chestnut hair had a hint of blond and tumbled gently on her shoulders. Most of all, she had a solid relationship with God, and it showed.

The doorbell to his apartment rang. He ran to open the door.

"Hi, Marcie! Come in."

The sight of her caught him off guard even though she had been on his mind all day. He could not wipe the grin from his face as he gave her a polite side hug and ushered her inside to a small sitting area with an old couch and an older brown leather chair.

Marcie sized up his place. Behind the couch where he'd asked her to sit, the wall had a window opening to the kitchen. The kitchen was small but worked perfectly for a pair of bachelors who were gone most of the day and rarely cooked. There was no TV in the living room, just a coffee table with a stack of Bible commentaries on top.

"How was your trip?" Jack asked.

"It went well."

"Good."

"Have you had a nice day?" Marcie asked.

"Yeah, I've had a very nice day."

"Good."

In the awkward silence that followed, Jack reached mentally for one of the twelve to fifteen potential conversation starters he had rehearsed for Marcie's arrival. But Marcie interrupted his train of thought.

20

"Jack, thanks so much for letting me come. I know it was last minute. I hope you didn't have to rearrange anything for me."

"Oh! It's no problem at all," he lied. "I'm glad you called."

After the initial hesitation, they quickly plunged past the small talk and caught each other up on how their friends were doing. Jack had picked out a pizza place off the beaten path for their dinner, so at a good break in the conversation, he suggested they head there before it got too late.

The restaurant was downtown, and Jack had to parallel park—something he was very proficient at doing. As he did so, he noticed that Marcie was not hugging the passenger's side door handle like she used to do on their dates at Harding. He jumped out of his side of the car, came around to hers, and opened her door. She took his strong hand gently as she gracefully got out of the car. Jack was careful not to hold her hand too long.

"How is teaching going?" Jack asked as they stepped together along the city sidewalk.

"Oh great! Except for the class bully. I'm not sure what to do about him."

Jack laughed. Her world was so different from his. It was refreshing.

In front of the restaurant was a small step up to the entrance. Marcie was so engrossed in talking about her students that she misjudged the height of the stair. Her foot hit the concrete hard as she tripped and caught herself with her other foot. Thankfully she was at the end of a sentence and there was a natural place to pause. She looked up quickly and to her relief, noticed that Jack was looking forward, seeming not to notice her misstep. She felt her face redden with slight embarrassment. She cleared her throat and finished telling her fourth grade news as they entered the restaurant.

The waiter seated them and took their drink orders. At a break in the conversation, Jack said, "How did you like the way I averted my eyes when you tripped?"

*That's Jack Jones for you. Nothing slips past him,* Marcie thought. *I should expect nothing less from the person who asked me if I wanted to "enter into a dating relationship" so formally last year.* In spite of herself, she laughed with Jack. She liked his laugh. It was a guttural laugh, emanating from his heart. When he laughed, his whole being was visibly joyful. She liked that. She felt very

21

comfortable and happy with him. Why did he seem taller to her tonight? St. Louis suited him. He was in his element here.

Dinner was wonderful, and Marcie found herself regretting that the evening came to an end so quickly. While they rode to the girls' house, where Jack had arranged for her to stay, Marcie shared that Judy, one of her housemates, had been driving her crazy with nagging remarks all the time. She was always reminding Marcie to do her share of the cleaning or asking her to run an extra errand on her way home from school. Frankly, she said, it cramped her style to try to cater to her finicky friend.

"Well," Jack said, "it sounds like you just need to serve her."

Marcie sat in silence as the gentle rebuke stung her unexpectedly. She couldn't believe he had just said those words to her. True enough, she was not putting Judy in a good light. And Jack had stopped her dead in her tracks and given her godly advice in the process! Her initial reaction of being indignant was conquered by her recognition that he was right. No one had ever talked to her like that before.

Jack moved the conversation to the topic of the girls' house. He told her who would be there that she knew from Harding. They pulled into a parking space in front of the large, beautiful, old, and slightly run-down antebellum home. Before she knew what was happening, Jack bid her good night.

---

Kelly, one of the interns with Jack at McAlister Road Church, showed Marcie around the house. It was huge with six bedrooms and four bathrooms. It reminded Marcie of a sorority house she'd seen once. She was to sleep in a room with Kelly and two other girls. The faces she recognized from Harding smiled back at her. Exhaustion suddenly hit her at the sight of a bed.

She went into the bathroom adjacent to the room where she was staying to brush her teeth. She could hear two girls talking in the bedroom on the other side of the bathroom from hers, even with the door closed. She couldn't resist eavesdropping. The first voice she heard seemed calmer than the second one.

"Oh, Casey, you know he didn't mean anything by it. I'm sure his reason was as good as he said it was. Jack is not the type to make up a story."

"Okay, but a random friend from out of town? All of a sudden? What if it's a girl?"

"Look, if you want to keep fretting over it, that's your problem. I think you and Jack make a great couple. Everyone said so the other night at the devotional."

"Really?"

"Yeah! You guys are so cute together. Jack is definitely at a point in his life where he needs to settle down. No guy *really* wants to go to the mission field alone. Jack's no exception. He needs you, Casey."

"I wish you were right. And I wish I could see him again this week. I miss him already."

"Hey, if Jack kisses a girl, then he's serious. He's not the kind of person to mess around. He's got a good reputation."

"I guess you're right. Well anyway, thanks so much for letting me crash here tonight. It's nice to get away from my folks' house and get a little girl time, especially when a boy is on my mind!"

Marcie's tired body suddenly felt a jolt of energy. They had to be talking about Jack Jones. But she couldn't investigate because she didn't know either one of these women. Not only that, but she felt that perhaps she was receiving her due punishment for having eavesdropped in the first place. *If only I had just turned the water on stronger*, she thought as she put toothpaste on her toothbrush. She had a feeling she would be awake for a while now.

*Why is that conversation bothering me so much?* Marcie wondered. *Apparently Jack does not know that this Casey, whoever she is, is spending the night here. Anyway, it doesn't matter because I certainly have no ulterior motive behind coming up to visit Jack. It's just a visit with a friend because I didn't have any other plans and didn't want to go home again for Thanksgiving. Right?*

She couldn't shake an unfamiliar uneasiness in her stomach. Maybe getting something to drink would help. She decided to head back toward the kitchen. As she exited through the second door that opened into the hallway, she was greeted almost too abruptly by a girl walking briskly down the hall.

"Oh, hi! My name is Morgan. I was hoping I might run into you. I've been wanting to meet you."

"Hello," Marcie managed to reply.

"Kelly told me that you are the one visiting Jack this weekend."

"Yeah. Just friends, but yeah." Marcie chided herself. *Why did I feel the need to specify?* She was flustered and annoyed at this girl's nosiness.

"Just friends? You mean he's not dating you or anything?"

"No, we're just friends from Harding," Marcie clarified again.

"Oh, okay. Well, I was thinking of asking Jack to come with me to a class reunion this year. I'm glad to know that he is still available. I certainly wouldn't want to step on toes. Jack is so cute, sweet, and spiritual! He's the perfect guy. And what can I say? I'm not shy, so why not? It's the seventies, after all."

"Oh, don't worry. You're not stepping on any toes. I'm sure Jack would be glad to go with you."

"You really think so?"

"Sure!"

*What in the world is going on here?* Marcie thought. *First of all, I have never met this girl before. So how could I possibly know if Jack would be glad to go with her? Second, and most disturbing, I do not want Jack going with her anywhere!* Maybe the day had worn her senses down. She definitely needed to get some rest. Jack had said he wanted to show her around tomorrow. Maybe she could hint around and get to the bottom of this side of Jack that she had never known before. She didn't know he had become so popular with the ladies.

Marcie pulled the sheet and blanket up over her chilled feet and legs. Wishing she had a bit of a heavier cover, she tucked the top of the thin quilt right under her chin. Then, curled up on her side, she closed her eyes and left the world of consciousness.

# CHAPTER 4

Wednesday morning, Marcie awoke to the thoughts of Jack with either Morgan or Casey still bothering her. Kelly had agreed to take Marcie with her up to McAlister Road after breakfast. Marcie was supposed to meet Jack there at eight o'clock. She dressed carefully, wanting to look good but not appear overdressed for a day with a friend.

When they arrived, Marcie saw Jack standing just outside the church's main entrance, talking with what looked to be an elder of the church. Seeing her, Jack excused himself and ushered Marcie over to his car.

Jack had told Marcie the night before that he had a hospital visit to make, and Marcie had accepted the invitation to go with him. They were to see Mike Fitts, who was recovering from surgery. After Jack explained that Mike Fitts was an elder at McAlister Road, there was a lull in the conversation.

"So did you feel comfortable enough last night?" Jack asked.

"Oh, yes. Everyone was very friendly. They all seemed to like you a lot."

Marcie was hoping for some insight into Jack's feelings about one or more of the girls there, but reading between the lines was not Jack's forte. He began telling her instead about miscellaneous church members and about some of his early experiences with them upon his arrival in St. Louis. Marcie listened and wondered how Jack was able to juggle all of his responsibilities at his Cutting Edge Photofinishing job and also the demands of serving as a minister at McAlister Road. Clearly God was at work in his life. It was very attractive to watch. She felt a desire to ask him more questions, suddenly realizing that she missed out on getting to know this side of him all those years at Harding. She had wasted so much time with other guys while a pretty great one had been in front of her all along.

When they arrived at the hospital, they entered through the front doors. Jack waved at the lady behind the desk and then led the way confidently to the elevators down the hall. The hospital was a maze to Marcie, and by the time they stepped off the elevator and into the post-op wing, she was truly lost. Jack, on the other hand, acted as if he had just walked from his bedroom to the kitchen.

Jack knocked on Mike's door and called, "Hello, Mike, it's Jack."

"Oh, come in, Jack! How nice of you to come!"

Jack quickly introduced Marcie and chatted easily with Mike as Marcie listened. She had never seen anyone Jack's age act the way he did around an invalid. She had tagged along many times with her father when he visited folks in the hospital. But Jack had a grace and smoothness about him that surprised her. He was different from her dad, and yet his style was good. He spoke to Mike with ease. There was no discomfort in his voice. She herself felt a bit tongue tied as she watched with growing interest this friend of hers minister to a man in a sick bed.

Toward the end of the visit, Jack took Mike's hand and asked him if he could pray for him. By the end of the prayer, Marcie's coolness toward Jack was completely gone. As they meandered back through the labyrinth of hallways toward the front doors, she regarded him with new interest. Sure, he was still just a friend, but she was proud to know him.

After a quick lunch, they headed to Jack's next appointment, which was a Bible study with a college student who had just started coming to church. He was hungry to hear more about Jesus. The two of them spent an hour reading and discussing the gospel of John while Marcie listened with new and growing interest.

After a little sightseeing and an early dinner, they went back to McAlister Road, where Jack taught the singles' class at church. It was obvious to Marcie that Jack was made for church ministry. He opened the Bible and brought a passage of Scripture to life. When he spoke, verses seemed to pop off the page. This particular night, he had chosen a passage from the Old Testament. He gave a quick history of the kings of Israel in order to arrive at Hezekiah's time. Marcie was impressed with the way he pronounced all of the Old Testament Hebrew names so perfectly. His knowledge impressed her. She was even more drawn to his obvious and radical love for God.

Everywhere they went that day, people wanted to talk to Jack. *How could Jack really know this many people?* Marcie wondered. She was amazed at how he handled the constant barrage of attention. She watched as he maneuvered his way through the crowd coolly, like a politician, and marveled at the way he laughed pleasantly at one remark while turning slowly to the next person at just the right time.

On the way back to the girls' house, Marcie was pensive. She gave Jack a quick goodnight and went straight to her room. Though other girls were in the house, she would have the bedroom to herself tonight. The three roommates had gone to their respective homes for the long weekend. All thoughts of the troubling conversation she'd overhead the night before about Jack were gone. She had just spent the entire day with Jack, and it had been wonderful.

She plopped down on the bed with her clothes on. Her thoughts quickly returned to Jack. What a guy. He was more handsome than she remembered. She thought about what his hand looked like when he held Mr. Fitts's hand to pray with him. *He has good hands,* she thought. Though they were together all day, he hadn't made any moves toward her at all. She respected that. Maybe he saw her as a friend and had no intentions of making a move. Or maybe . . .

She decided to skip brushing her teeth. So tired. What was tomorrow again? She would have to call her mother and wish her a happy Thanksgiving. Hers was certainly going to be a happy one.

---

The weeks and months that followed Marcie's visit to St. Louis were a wonderful blur of romantic bliss for Jack. Somehow after she had returned home from the weekend, he had mustered up the courage to ask her out again and found she was responding differently to him. Dating her, though, was an emotional roller coaster and anything but smooth. He was on the ride of his life, and he soon became wiser. Whenever a problem arose that threatened their relationship, his nonchalance always won her back. She was drawn to the bold, confident, strong man that he had become. He could hardly believe, after he'd sunk so low in self-doubt, that God had rewarded him not only with a clear path to the mission field but also with the woman of his dreams.

It had taken her a while, but Marcie eventually came around to "entering into a dating relationship" with Jack Jones after all. God never ceased to amaze her. He had shielded her from desiring him too soon so that they would find each other at just the right time in their lives.

One sunny day in April, Jack took Marcie for a walk in a park near his apartment. The azaleas and rhododendrons were just beginning to bud. Bluebirds were looking for nesting spots and warbling across the red cedars to each other. Jack's stomach was in his throat. He knew what he wanted to ask Marcie but was unsure of how she would respond. Although he had gained her trust, he still feared that if he came on too strong, he might turn her away for good. But he couldn't hold back any longer. He concentrated on maintaining a calm exterior. He would need it for what he was about to do.

As they rested on a park bench, Marcie placed her head on Jack's shoulder. She felt so happy when she was with him. She wanted to spend the rest of her life with him. She could feel his heart beating rapidly beneath his collared shirt. He said her name in a strange, hesitant voice. She raised her head, wondering what was about to transpire.

"Marcie," he said again, "I want to share a Scripture passage with you."

"Okay," she said quietly. She was used to him opening up the Bible to her, but she sensed that something was different this time.

"It's from Proverbs 30, verses 18 and 19. 'Three things are too wonderful for me; four I do not understand: the way of an eagle in the sky, the way of a serpent on a rock, the way of a ship on the high seas, and the way of a man with a maiden.'" He paused, took her hand, and said, "Marcie, I want you to be my maiden."

Marcie sat glued to the bench as the reality of the moment washed over her. She felt a surge of emotion rise up and fill her to the brim. The words that she had dreamed of hearing all of her life were about to be spoken to her.

"Marcie, will you marry me?" he said.

Her entire face beamed with her answer. "Yes!"

Jack placed a ring on her finger, and she threw her arms around him with embracing confirmation as she drank in Jack, the day, and her ring. She tossed a glance up at the heavens and knew God was smiling on them.

After a few minutes, Jack took her hand, and they began to make their way to the park exit. Suddenly they noticed a large bird flying overhead. It looked a lot like an eagle. It swooped down briefly right in front of them, hesitated, and then disappeared into the azure, cloudless sky. A few steps later, they gasped as a snake slithered across the path in front of them. The eagle and snake reminded them both of the verse from Proverbs. They arrived at the pond just inside the park entrance and watched several small boys sailing toy boats. Their thoughts turned again to the words of the proverb Jack had read: "The way of an eagle in the sky, the way of a snake on a rock, the way of a ship on the high seas, and the way of a man with a maiden." They looked at each other, seeing in the other one the fulfillment of the last bit of the proverb—the way of a man with a maiden. Neither dared speak.

Already their souls were becoming one. God was moving them right along on the path He'd made in advance for them to follow. Life together would be an adventure. And though to many, being in the center of God's will might be the most terrifying place in all the world, to Marcie and Jack there was no place they would rather be.

# PART II

# A Mission Is Born

# CHAPTER 5

"Fasten your seatbelts and prepare for takeoff," announced the voice over the intercom. Marcie held her sleeping toddler close to her breast and felt Jack squeeze her arm. Their destination: Geneva, Switzerland.

As the plane lifted off the runway, she looked out her window at the wing of the aircraft. She watched it move upward and turn into the sky as the aileron at the edge of the airplane wing moved downward. Her thoughts drifted back over the past two years of her newlywed life.

Their short, six-week engagement had flown by in a blink, with barely enough time to plan the wedding details. Thankfully Marcie's two sisters and mother had rushed in to the rescue. Her thoughts clouded for a moment at the reminder that she was moving far away from her family. But when memories of the actual ceremony popped into her head, she grinned. They had decided that they wanted their wedding to be a simple celebration. She smiled as she remembered her dress—a bit too short—and the cake, the guests, and then the honeymoon. She and Jack were so sunburned after their trip to Greer's Ferry Lake in northern Arkansas that it took practically an entire week to recover from the blisters. When they returned to their little apartment in St. Louis, tired but happy, they plunged into their first argument as a married couple. Marcie laughed at the memory.

"What do you mean, you invited Mike over for dinner tonight?"

"Honey, I didn't think you would mind having such a close friend over. And besides, he wants to talk to me about the new mission team he's putting together."

"Jack, I appreciate how much you love this man and all of the people that you work with, for that matter. But next time, you are going to have to give me more time to prepare! Is this what I need to expect from you all the time? Last minute plans?"

"Well, I expected to be able to invite someone over if I wanted to. After all, I am a minister, and that is what ministers are supposed to do, right?"

"That is what they are supposed to do *if* they have checked in with their wives and received approval first! Especially if it happens to be the night after their honeymoon!"

Marcie remembered Jack's laugh, how he pulled her into his arms and asked for her forgiveness, and how she melted in his embrace. As the plane leveled after its ascent, she thought about the many different adjustments she'd had to make since marrying Jack Jones, the minister. Privacy, she learned quickly, was not a privilege to be taken for granted. She and Jack often opened their home to individuals who needed help. Sometimes the invitation was for a simple meal, but sometimes it included sharing their humble home with someone for more than just one night.

Adding their first child to the mix had not been easy either. Neither she nor Jack was prepared for the degree of anxiety that colic could bestow upon a family. She remembered sobbing night after night, wondering what she was doing wrong to have a baby that cried so much.

MaryAnna, now a year and a half old, squirmed in Marcie's arms as if she could sense her thoughts and was just as relieved as her mommy that those days were over. Marcie patted her baby girl's back gently and stroked her soft blond curls. Oh, those were such difficult times, but she felt much stronger, braver, and closer to Jack for having overcome them with him. After MaryAnna's birth, Jack's original request for twelve children had quickly gone down to six. And as if on cue, she had gotten pregnant again, in late March, a few months before their departure to Geneva. Thank goodness for just enough time to recover from morning sickness before this trip overseas. Holding her sleeping toddler, feeling the first movements of an unborn child inside her womb, and riding off into adventure at the side of the man of her dreams, Marcie felt like the richest woman in the world.

MaryAnna slept most of the way to Geneva. Jack and Marcie tried to rest too, but excitement kept them from sleeping very deeply. By the time they landed at the airport in Zurich around noon, they felt exhausted.

A few weeks before their departure from St. Louis, Jack had communicated briefly with the missionary family they were going to be working with, Ben and Amy Wilson. The Wilsons were not moving to Geneva until the following week, but Jack had wanted to get there as soon as possible and was thrilled to find an earlier flight. He loved discovering new places and getting a feel for the territory.

34

Reading maps and the challenge of exploring sights unseen thrilled him to no end. The plan was that the Wilsons and the Joneses would work with a local church that was ten years old. During their time there, they would seek guidance about where to launch a church on their own.

———————

Initially Jack and Marcie lived in a hotel room in downtown Geneva. It was barely big enough for them. Conservation of space was important in Europe. Sprawling land and large houses as in the United States, ranch-style homes, shopping malls, and football stadiums were sparse there, where history went back centuries, even millennia. People were stacked up on top of each other in apartment buildings, subways, and city buses.

The hotel room they chose offered a bed, a crib for MaryAnna, and a bathroom. It was simple but enough. The hotel building, near the downtown center between a bank and a travel agency, was modern for the day—completely concrete and rather dull to look at from the outside, mostly gray with faded yellow borders around the windows and doorframes. The decor inside was very basic: fake flowers at the check-in desk, the aged hall carpet a muted burgundy and green paisley, and a framed painting of a plant or animal typifying the region between each door. But like everything else in Geneva, it was very clean.

Whenever they entered after excursions into the city, it seemed the concierge always had a remark they could have done without—either about their accents, their staying so long, or MaryAnna getting into mischief. They much preferred their interactions with the janitor, who filled them in on all of the cheap restaurants in the area and even threw in some useful suggestions of things to do with a toddler. It was thanks to him that they learned the names of many of the nearby parks, although Jack probably would have discovered them on his own eventually, as he studied the map of the city while drinking his breakfast coffee and again every evening before bed.

Each morning Jack and Marcie savored the cup of Swiss coffee, fresh croissants, and bread waiting for them on one of the three lobby tables. They were glad to give up their usual St. Louis bacon and eggs for the soft-on-the-inside, crunchy-on-the-outside goodness of these breakfast treats, available fairly cheaply while they stayed at the Hotel Royal. After breakfast they began the day with a half a mile stroll to the nearest tramway stop followed by either scoping out possible apartments to live in, searching for grocery stores, or tackling more boring endeavors such as obtaining driver's licenses, registering for student visas, changing out money, and the like. They tried to see as many sights as they could. The Gothic and Romanesque architecture of the cathedrals was enthralling to them. The stained glass images were entrancing. Yet Jack and Marcie reflected that the pictures of Jesus seemed sadly removed from the reality of the Jesus they knew personally. He was not a distant person to be accessed only through such cold, stone-built structures.

Before leaving the States, Jack and Marcie had sold most of their expensive wedding gifts. Trimming down their material goods had made their move simpler and alleviated some financial pressure by providing extra spending money. They had to eat out almost every night while they lived in the hotel. Unfortunately, most Swiss restaurants were not exactly toddler friendly, and they had to wait at least thirty minutes for their food to arrive. Although the food was second to none, they found it difficult to let their palates savor the succulence of *boeuf bourgignon* with a squirming toddler. MaryAnna would sit still to eat only if it could be done in under fifteen minutes or if it involved cookies or French fries—which were never on the above-par menus of the local café restaurants. So most of the time they would settle for a pizzeria or some place serving *croques monsieurs* (toasted ham and cheese sandwiches).

The city of Geneva was extremely clean. During their morning excursions, it was not uncommon for them to see city street workers hosing down the sidewalks, picking up trash, or sweeping and bagging leaves and debris. Paid employees were not the only ones keeping the city looking squeaky-clean. The Joneses were surprised to see locals frequently picking up paper or candy wrappers, disposing of them in conveniently placed trash receptacles. The people's practice of picking up and throwing away trash would eventually lead some to see the local Church of Christ flyer and come to discover what faith is all about.

The physical beauty of Geneva was postcard perfect. In the spring and summer, blooming geraniums, zinnias, and marigolds hung in baskets under apartment windows. Their perfume wafted through the air. High above the tallest buildings, the Alps cut into the sky, a perfect backdrop to the city, trying to remind Geneva's apathetic inhabitants of who created them in the first place.

The resident missionaries the Joneses were assigned to work with initially, Steve and Janice Mulberry, showed them around all of the touristy places. Their city overview was complete with the *Jet d'eau* flower clock, St. Peter's cathedral, *La Place Neuve,* and *Place Bourg du Four.*

Jack and Marcie eventually moved from the hotel and settled into a third floor apartment in downtown Geneva. It was a relief to be able to move what little furniture they had shipped over with them into their two-bedroom residence. Their fellow missionaries, Ben and Amy Wilson, rented on the first floor of the same building.

---

Marcie and Jack discovered that their college French classes did not prepare them for the real French world. As they worked on their French-speaking ability, they learned from masters who wouldn't wait for them to study for the test: the Swiss people, with real, culturally shocking personalities not found in textbooks. Some Swiss tolerated Americans well enough, but others had little patience for accent-ridden amateurs trying to integrate themselves into unfamiliar surroundings. The language barrier was crippling in presenting the gospel as well as in regular life challenges.

One night MaryAnna woke up with a stomach virus. After several days with no apparent improvement in MaryAnna, Marcie and Jack took her to a doctor recommended by the Mulberrys. Diagnosing her with a nasty flu, the doctor told them they would just have to wait for the sickness to run its course. Marcie was fearful that MaryAnna was dehydrated and was desperate to do something to ease her child's discomfort. She asked the doctor if he was sure that nothing could be done. Aside from recommending lots of fluids, he gave her another negative response and told her they could go home. After the doctor had exited the examination room, Marcie asked the nurse if it would make a difference if they were native Swiss and if the doctor would send a Swiss child who was as sick as hers to the hospital. To Marcie's horror, the nurse replied that he probably would have.

Anger and resentment flooded Marcie as she ranted to Jack on the way home. "What are we doing here? Do you think that God really wants our baby to suffer? Jack, I knew that you and I would have to sacrifice, but I didn't expect God to allow our innocent daughter to suffer at the hands of these stuck-up, self-absorbed, arrogant ingrates!"

Jack's heart was heavy. The silence following Marcie's outburst was palpable. Her arms were folded furiously, and her chin quivered in anger. This was not how they pictured mission work. Jack knew it would be difficult. But now he had his first moment of doubt. *What if I misread God? Shouldn't God be rewarding us for following after Him instead of giving us more trials?*

Anger seeped into his thoughts as well. With MaryAnna's every cry, he felt a new surge of irritation. Inside he railed against their circumstances, which he could do nothing about. He struggled with the reality of endangering his own child. The verse from the book of James about counting suffering all joy felt inapplicable. His thoughts whirled around inside, tormenting him. He knew he needed to pray, but he found it difficult. *Isn't this wonderful,* he thought sarcastically. *The missionary who has a hard time praying.* So troubled were his thoughts that at first he didn't notice that MaryAnna was settling down. Her whimpering had stopped. Traffic was awful, and it was raining. Marcie was silent but obviously still fuming.

For the next twenty-four hours, MaryAnna continued to throw up everything that they tried to put in her mouth. Jack spent hours reading her stories in bed. Finally they decided they should take her to the hospital themselves. There, after another consult with a physician, they decided to stay overnight so they could make sure she didn't get too dehydrated. When the Swiss sun rose on the beautiful city of Geneva the next day, Jack and Marcie were completely haggard and bleary-eyed. Instead of coffee, Jack sipped a bottle of cola while he read his lethargic daughter yet another story. As soon as he dozed off, he was startled by his own daughter's voice.

"Daddy, ah dink," MaryAnna mumbled and reached for the bottle in Jack's hand.

"No, sweet girl," Jack coaxed. "You can't have Daddy's drink. It might hurt your tummy again." But it was too late.

MaryAnna had managed to pull the drink out of her Daddy's exhausted hand and take a big sip.

"No!" Jack shouted, frustrated and wide awake. He reached for the trash can to get ready for the inevitable regurgitation.

MaryAnna handed the cola back to her daddy and smiled weakly. "I coke, Daddy."

Minutes went by, and MaryAnna's cheeks took on a tiny tinge of color. The soda was like godly medicine to the child. For the first time in almost a week, MaryAnna kept the liquid down. When two hours had passed and the nurse came to check on them, Jack exploded with the news.

"She is going to be okay!" he beamed. "The cola helped her! So much for traditional medicine, huh?"

He laughed out loud.

"You should not have done that!" the French nurse scolded in English with a strong accent. She softened when she observed her patient obviously turning the corner on the sickness. "*C'est incroyable*" ("It's incredible").

Presently the doctor entered. "It is a strange coincidence," he said. "Cola could never cure a sickness. It is unheard of."

Jack spoke with confidence. "Oh, no, sir. With all due respect, the cola did not cure my child. God did."

The doctor and nurse rolled their eyes at each other and smiled patronizingly, choosing to ignore the crazy American. But Jack didn't care. Never before in his life had he been so thankful to God for good health. He knew in his heart that God was sending him a signal, confirming his call overseas. He would not grow weary or faint of heart. God would be with him and his family.

---

Once the family was settled into the apartment, Jack's daily routine began with a strong cup of Swiss coffee followed by a 15-minute commute to the church building to study, to meet with Steve Mulberry and Ben Wilson to discuss the next church meeting, or to pray. Sometimes the three of them would have a Bible study with a church member. Other times they would brainstorm about how to attract new members.

Marcie stayed busy with housework and home life. Occasionally she would put MaryAnna's shawl on her and they would set off hand-in-hand into the yonder of civilized French-ness mixed with German-ness and a little something unique to Geneva too. Marcie quickly became more proficient with her French. The locals liked her accent, and she noticed that if people didn't smile at her, then they would usually smile at her blonde-haired, blue-eyed daughter.

MaryAnna flashed grins to the young and old alike. It didn't matter to her who pinched her cheeks or helped her up and down stairs when her very pregnant mother became too uncomfortable to do so.

For Marcie, MaryAnna had become a natural bridge in a grown-up world. She found she was beginning to feel comfortable in her new homeland. She loved the fresh produce and flowers so readily available in open-air markets. The intoxicating scent of vine-ripened tomatoes, juicy plums, round apples, and green peppers was always enough to lure her to the morning farmers' markets. She would indulge her senses in the pleasure of Swiss agriculture at its finest. A robust, girthy farmer would salute her in French: "*Bonjour, Madame.*" With the good kind of dirt under his fingernails, he would select the most beautiful of his wares for her to sample. Marcie had little resistance for the spell that proper Swiss food cast over her.

Life was simpler here than back home. The practicality of the Swiss was refreshing. Although they were fashionable, it was common to see folks wear the same clothes for a few days in a row. *Long live body odor and extra time to sit in a street café!* she thought. Her "hippy" tendencies from her college days merged perfectly with this newfound motto. Switzerland was an ironic mix of base humanness and intellectual snobbery. There was something attractive about the marriage of uppity and plain.

Marcie longed for God's truth to break into the somber faces of the Swiss people. They seemed glazed over from boredom with life. She prayed every night that God would send new converts to the small church she and Jack were now a part of. She wanted so much for the people to have the same joy in Christ that she and Jack possessed. In spite of the alienation they had felt when MaryAnna was so sick, they were beginning to see how God could use them here, and they trusted that God would protect them from harm.

# CHAPTER 6

Jack held his newborn baby boy for the first time on December 22, 1977, at 3:30 a.m. He paced up and down the hospital halls, talking to his son, Isaac Daniel. He told him they were on a mission from God to help the people here in Switzerland to turn to Jesus. He told him about his big sister and about his mother, who was so brave to give birth to him in a place where she had just learned to speak the language. He was filled with emotion. Seeing Marcie suffer through this childbirth had brought him to his knees, literally. He had passed out briefly when it was time for her to push. Marcie amazed him. She was by far the bravest woman he had ever known. The fact that God had given her to him as his wife still baffled him.

MaryAnna turned two years old the day after Isaac was born. In Swiss hospitals, it was customary for new mothers to stay for a week postpartum. During this time, Jack stayed at home with MaryAnna and visited Marcie and Isaac frequently during the day. A few days after Marcie and Isaac's release from the hospital, Jack was to preach his first sermon in French. He was nervous but excited. He had written out everything just as he wanted to say it.

The small church in Geneva where they attended had been planted a decade before the Joneses' and Wilsons' arrival. Almost thirty people came fairly regularly. The most regular ones were two married couples in their fifties and three single older ladies in their sixties or seventies. A single mom with a four-year-old boy and a young twenty-year-old student had started coming after Jack and Marcie arrived in Geneva. The others were middle aged. Some were married and some weren't. Some worked and some were unemployed. More than a few smoked one last cigarette just before entering, giving the meeting room a hint of secondhand smoke, usually overcome by the aroma from the church coffee pot.

Steve Mulberry, the preacher, had hosted several door-knocking campaigns during which American Christians would come on short mission trips to help. Most of the current church members had connected with the church through these campaigns. Steve had also set up several Bible correspondence courses for new believers. Jack had taken over many of the studies, and even though the communication was mostly written, it helped to boost his confidence in speaking French.

The anticipated Sunday for Jack's first sermon arrived at last. It was still too soon for Marcie to venture out with Isaac, so she stayed home with the children while Jack went to the church an hour early in order to pray and collect his thoughts. Françoise, a lady in her sixties, arrived first. Jack tried to chat with her as proficiently as he possibly could. Soon others joined them, and each one found a brown metal folding chair to sit in for the morning service. Steve Mulberry began with prayer, then announced in French, "Jack Jones will be speaking to us today for the first time. I look forward to hearing what God has laid on his heart to tell us." Everyone smiled. A few chuckled, and Françoise turned toward Jack with a proud, grandmother-like glance over her bifocals while she wheezed a smoky laugh.

Jack was anxious for his moment to arrive. The song service began with "*Oh, Fait de Mon Coeur*" ("Oh, Make of My Heart"), a selection from the light blue paperback songbook the church used as a hymnal that had been printed just a few years prior. It was bound in a black plastic spiral with the front and back made of a piece of laminated construction paper. It contained about 150 French hymns. One of Jack's favorites was sung next, "*Vers Toi, Seigneur*," a French translation of "Unto Thee, Oh Lord" from Psalm 25.

After the fourth song was sung, there was a short pause and then a discreet nod from Steve. Jack stood up in front of the group and looked out over the small crowd gathered. In a brief second, he realized that he was living the dream that was born in his spirit during his senior year at Harding.

"*Bonjour,*" he began confidently. After a few carefully planned words of welcome, he instructed that Bibles be opened to Proverbs 13:24. He read the passage in well-enunciated French. "He who spares the rod hates his son, but he who loves him is diligent to discipline him." He then shared a funny anecdote about how he had disciplined MaryAnna last week when she snuck into the kitchen one day and stole a piece of American candy he and Marcie had kept hidden in a special place. The image of sweet little MaryAnna getting into trouble made everyone laugh endearingly.

"*Oh, c'est pas vrai*" ("it's not true"), Françoise exclaimed in playful protest.

42

Jack went on to talk about how God the Father disciplines His children for their own good. He made several analogies about what "the rod" of discipline could symbolize in their lives. Somewhere along the way, he noticed that Françoise, though a frequent smiler and nodder, seemed unusually tickled. At first he dismissed it as something between her and her friend Dominique. But he then noticed that not only was Dominique also chuckling quietly to herself, but Mary France, along with her husband who had finally come that day, were both grinning from ear to ear as well. Somewhat frazzled, he looked down at his notes to be sure that he hadn't lost his place. He decided to plug on ahead, hoping that whatever inside joke was circulating among them would fizzle out shortly.

He cleared his throat and continued with his next point about practical ways that parents could discipline children. Finally, he wrapped up the sermon with his concluding statement: *"Alors comme nous avons lu dans ce verset de Proverbes, il est quelque fois nécèssaire d'utiliser notre vierge pour discipliner nos enfants."*

At this point, laughter released in the room like champagne popping off the cork. The people were beside themselves. Some were wiping their eyes from hysteria. Dumbfounded and uncomfortable, he stammered a question about what was so funny. Finally Françoise, dabbing her eyes with a *mouchoir* (hankerchief), pointed out that though the verse said to use a rod (*verge*) to discipline children, Jack had in fact used the word *vierge*, which to Jack's mortification did not mean rod at all but virgin. So in his final statement, he mistakenly had said, "As we read in the verse from Proverbs, it is sometimes necessary to use our virgin to discipline our children." His entire face turned the color of his crimson, button-up shirt. He smiled and then, letting the tension go, laughed with everyone.

As the post-service fellowship time was coming to a close and nearly everyone had headed home, Steve joked with Jack about his first language blunder as a missionary. Laughing, they both stepped outside with Bertrand, the twenty-something single student who had very much enjoyed Jack's lesson, especially the embarrassing mishap.

Jack drove his two-door Fiat home, reliving the mistake in torturous detail. When he arrived home, he wanted to tell Marcie what had happened but found that their small haven of an apartment was not peaceful today. Isaac was screaming to be fed, and Marcie, holding Isaac in one arm, was trying to help MaryAnna out of the bathroom with her other hand, exclaiming all the while, "MaryAnna, you are a big girl. You know that you are not supposed to wet your pants!"

As Jack closed the door behind him, he heard MaryAnna whimper, "I'm sorry, Mommy! I didn't mean to." The two-year-old's voice trailed off into loud wails.

"It's okay," said Marcie. "Mommy loves you. Just try to do better next time."

MaryAnna wiped her eyes and breathed heavily as she settled down. "Daddy!" she shouted suddenly at the sight of Jack. She ran half dressed toward him and jumped up in his arms.

Marcie brushed the hair out of her exhausted face, managing a weak smile. "How did things go this morning?"

"Oh, okay," was all he said, deciding the details could wait until later.

That night he put Isaac in the small bassinet next to his and Marcie's bed. He gazed down at the tiny hands, formed perfectly. Having meditated on the Proverbs verse of his sermon that day for so long, he thought of the lessons he felt God had revealed to him. It was hard to believe he might have to spank such a precious, helpless being someday. God was such a mystery. How could He give such amazing bundles of joy and then allow them to become imperfect and to require discipline?

He finally told Marcie about what happened while they ate a late dinner brought over by Jan Mulberry. Perhaps it was the exhaustion from having been up every two hours the night before to nurse Isaac, but as Marcie listened, she couldn't help but laugh hysterically when he came to the punch line about disciplining children with a virgin. Jack exploded with guffaws himself and thought of a neighboring verse. "A cheerful heart is a good medicine" (Proverbs 17:22).

# CHAPTER 7

Ben Wilson, Jack's missionary partner from the States, was a tall, gangly man. He appeared soft-spoken and almost shy at first meeting, but he radiated warmth and genuine kindness if given a chance. He was an all-American-looking guy and didn't seem to have any interest in giving up his baseball caps and bright white Nike brand shoes for the darker, more somber Swiss look. His handshake was gentle yet firm. If ever there were a missionary mold, Jack thought, Ben was it. He prayed fervently and loved the Lord passionately. Jack could not have asked for a more perfect coworker. The two of them got along very well, without even the slightest disputes. Ben seemed enthusiastic about whatever Jack suggested. And when Ben had ideas, Jack was more than happy to go along with him too. It was a tremendous blessing for Jack to have an honest person such as Ben on his side.

Ben and his wife, Amy, were a few years younger than the Joneses, but they were just as eager to make a difference in the lives of the Swiss people. Amy was quiet and reserved, but she was a true flower child of the 60s. She and Ben had an only child, a four-year-old named Debbie. Although Ben and Jack got along perfectly in their missionary work, the way Amy and Ben and Jack and Marcie parented their children was sometimes a source of tension between the mothers. Marcie viewed Amy as overindulging, and Amy viewed Marcie as too strict.

Amy was an environmentalist. She was known to put ice cubes back in the freezer to be reused if they had not completely melted in a drink. The Swiss habit of wearing the same clothes three or four days in a row suited her just fine. It was one of the rules to which she insisted that little Debbie adhere. She made Debbie brush her teeth without the water on and even trained her to take a very shallow bath, with barely enough water to cover up her legs.

Amy had the French language mastered better than Ben, Marcie, and Jack combined. She was very intelligent but had given up any career aspirations in favor of the call to come alongside her husband to the mission field. She was attractive in a hippy kind of way, and the Swiss people liked her earthy appeal. Though they differed about parenting, she and Marcie had their love of the Lord and mission work in common.

A year had gone by since Jack preached his famous "virgin sermon," and the Joneses and the Wilsons were beginning to feel the tug to move to France. It seemed their launching time was upon them. At the forefront of their minds, surfacing from the many prayer-filled nights, were two potential destination cities: Strasbourg and Nantes.

One evening in March 1979, Ben and Amy gathered with Jack and Marcie in the Joneses' living room to pray for direction. They sought God's guidance. Neither couple had a strong opinion about which city ought to be chosen. They just wanted to go where God needed them the most. Jack volunteered to travel to the two cities under consideration. The others agreed in prayer with him on the plan. Jack set out by train one bright morning soon thereafter, headed to Strasbourg first.

Early that same afternoon, after Amy had gotten Debbie down for her afternoon nap and was sipping some water with recycled ice while finishing off a leftover sandwich for lunch, Ben sat down at the kitchen table with her.

"Amy, let's pray for Jack again."

"Are you worried about him?"

"No. I just want to pray that God will make it blatantly obvious where we need to go. I want to pray for a sign."

Amy bowed her head immediately and waited for Ben to start.

"Father," Ben prayed, "please bless Jack. Please send someone his way, Lord. We want to boldly ask you to make it obvious to us all where we are supposed to go. Please send Jack a clear sign, a person even, something that he absolutely cannot miss. In Jesus' name we pray, Amen."

---

Strasbourg, while located in France, had a distinct German flair due to its proximity to the border between France and Germany. The city was annexed to the German empire in 1871. It became French again in 1919, after World War I, as a result of the Treaty of Versailles. Annexed again to Germany in 1940, it returned to its French roots once more in November of 1944, thanks to General Leclerc.

Upon arriving, Jack bypassed all of the quaint, vintage chalet-style buildings with flower box vases under the windows and headed straight for the nearest hole-in-the-wall coffee shop. With his *grand crème* in hand, he sat outside on the street, alongside a handful of other patrons. After one sip, he couldn't withhold a satisfactory smile as the concoction slid down into his gut, filling up his senses with a happiness he couldn't explain. He convinced himself that this might be the only addiction worth having.

He began to ponder his quest. Where would God lead him this time? "Lord," he prayed silently, "please make it clear."

Absentmindedly he watched people come and go. He nearly spilled his prized drink on himself when he realized suddenly that someone was looking right at him. It was someone familiar. He remembered having met the man at the men's retreat in Geneva, a man from France, but Jack couldn't remember which town.

*"Bonjour, Jacques! Je suis Serge."*

*"Oui, bonjour, Serge!"* Jack responded, leaning over to greet him with the culturally appropriate *bise*, a kiss cheek to cheek on each side. Jack was still taken aback by the fact that men did this to each other. He missed the personal space of the American handshake.

Serge accepted Jack's invitation to sit down and in French, jumped right into interview mode. "How is church work going in Geneva?"

"It is going very well," Jack replied, hesitant to reveal that he was seeking new territory at present. "We are really enjoying Geneva, and we thank God for moving us there."

"Are you coming to Nantes?" Serge asked boldly.

Jack remembered then that Nantes was Serge's hometown.

"As a matter of fact, I am on my way there tomorrow."

"Good," Serge responded simply. "We need you."

The rest of the conversation was a blur. Jack found himself sitting alone again with an empty coffee cup, watching Serge disappear into the crowd. No sooner had he prayed for a sign than Serge had appeared. And as quickly as he had come, he was gone. He called Ben immediately. After relating the story, there was a strange silence on the phone.

"Ben?"

"Uh, what time did this conversation take place?" Ben stammered at last.

"What time?" *Of all things to ask,* Jack thought. "Oh, I don't know. About 1:00 or 1:30. Why?"

"Well, around 1:30, Amy and I prayed that God would give us a clear sign as to where our team should go. We asked that He make it blatantly obvious to us all."

Jack hadn't expected an answer so quickly. But it was becoming very hard to resist the conviction that they were supposed to move to Nantes. He thanked Ben for the prayers, and told him that he would call again from Nantes the next day.

---

That night Jack stayed in a hotel in Strasbourg and the next morning boarded the train to Nantes. After the events of the day before, he opened his mind's eye even more to what God was trying to show him. As he rode the Nantes city bus from one stop to the next, discovering various historical locations, he watched the pedestrians and the car riders, children, teenagers, adults, and senior citizens. The French people stirred a sense of wonder in him. They had a story that he wanted to discover. Many of the faces he looked into were handsome and confident. They carried themselves with poise, with a sense that they didn't care what anyone thought about them. He rediscovered why his own people had so much respect for the French in spite of the political rifts between them. The French culture had many qualities that Americans regarded highly. France was the "cool uncle" from cosmopolitan Europe.

The disposition of the French was refreshing to Jack. There were beggars, there were those who seemed to have it all together, and there was a wide range in between. While some flaunted fashion with boldness and style and others dressed in more ordinary clothes, all seemed comfortable with their look. They were not insecure or self-conscious. At the same time, there was a distant look in their eyes, one that made Jack wonder what had happened to them. That look, which Jack labeled sadness, was mysterious to him. Many worked cigarettes in and out of their mouths and tapped the ashes onto the ground with experience. All of them were so distinctly French, and their language suited them well. Their mouths didn't have to open as wide as Americans with rounded vowel sounds (especially Southerners and Texans, which Jack and Marcie were).

Jack found himself longing to enter into their lives and help them find Jesus. He knew without a doubt that he and Marcie and Ben and Amy were supposed to move to Nantes. He felt the fire ignite within him. These were the people God wanted them to reach.

---

Although the call was clear, it took the team almost a year to make the transition from Geneva to Nantes. They had to talk to the Mulberry family, who were very sad at the prospect of losing these two families in their ministry at the Geneva Church of Christ but understood and supported their calling. Letters had to be written to supporting churches back home, and in some cases phone calls had to be made. And then there were logistical issues to be resolved such as finding homes and a church location. It was late February in 1980 when the Joneses and the Wilsons were finally able to settle into their place of calling.

Marcie loved their house at *3, Rue des Magnoliers*. Because it was still winter when they moved, the crepe myrtle on the side of their house showed no signs of life yet. Nor did the beautiful magnolia tree in the front. In the back of the house was a nice-sized yard, much bigger than most in the neighborhood. The landlord had planted several different types of flowers, bushes, and trees throughout. Marcie would soon find that each week in the spring would reveal a new flowering surprise. Her favorite would be the blue hydrangeas that bloomed all summer along the north side of the house. The house itself had three small bedrooms upstairs. The kitchen floor was tiled in large, black-and-white squares. The family room was small but functional. And to top it off, the house was located close to the elementary school.

Both she and Jack were thankful to be on the other side of town from Ben and Amy, so as to spread themselves out across the city. Two single girls from the U.S. would soon be joining their small team: Kathy Fitzgerald and Alice King. The two were coming as interns for a year's time, and they would be staying in an apartment together in downtown Nantes. Kathy was coming from Jack's home church, McAlister Road. Alice was coming from a church in California. She had only become a Christian a few years earlier, but to the sending church, she seemed on fire for spreading God's word across the world. She had found out about the mission in

Nantes through a friend. Both Kathy and Alice had majored in French in college, so they were eager to learn to communicate quickly and get right to work.

---

Two-year-old Isaac and four-year-old MaryAnna Jones had every intention of helping their mom unpack boxes in their new home. However, the extent of their work was to pull out all of the toys and hop into the boxes she unpacked to make playhouses out of them.

A few days after the move, Marcie started noticing that in the mornings, if Jack got the coffee percolating before she woke up, she had a queasy feeling in her stomach. At first she thought maybe she just wasn't getting enough sleep because of the move, all of the excitement, and the children waking up too early every morning. But when lettuce and chicken began to make her feel sick, she suspected something else.

Jack was thrilled to find out that another baby was on the way. With Isaac's birth, his original goal of twelve children, which had diminished to six after MaryAnna's arrival, had slipped down to four. But he was still just as excited as the first two pregnancies to hold a precious new little one. Marcie was excited too, but she couldn't show it for another three months because of the morning sickness. Were they always going to be transitioning during her times of gestation? The fixing up of the house that she was looking forward to doing quickly became a chore. She decided to put everything on hold until she felt better. Her visions of curtains, flower pots, and photos hanging on walls turned into half-opened boxes and piles of clothes everywhere as the reality of child number three forming in her womb settled upon her.

Jack and Ben were busy most days trying to complete the business side of moving. Once their families were officially moved in, they immediately set about the task of finding a church meeting place. They found an old office building near the center of town at *10, Rue de la Fosse*. The place had been gutted and used as a warehouse for the past few years. With some new flooring and a few other tasteful touches, they felt it would be very suitable for a church plant. They purchased the obligatory metal folding chairs, new carpet, and of course, a church coffee pot. They were used to meeting every Tuesday night as a team to pray, so they decided to begin a Bible study on Tuesday nights at the *salle*—pronounced *"sahl"*— a word meaning *room* in French, which is what they called the church building. Their goal was to each invite at least one person by the first meeting, set for the last Sunday in February 1980.

They racked their brains together as to whom they could invite first. When one of them invited the postman, in American accented French, he sloughed the invitation off with, *"Non merci. Je n'ai pas besoin de religion Americaine."* They politely ignored his remark about not needing American religion. Being American had been somewhat of a hurdle to overcome in Geneva, but it was an obelisk to get past here in France. In response to their gestures of friendship, they were often patronized with simple tips about where they could go for help and how to get to the tourist office—and those were the nice suggestions. A few they approached took advantage of the opportunity to rant about Americans being wasteful, fat, materialistic, and sticking their noses in other people's business. The language was colorful too. It was not without a great amount of difficulty that these four young missionaries invited five people who seemed at least somewhat interested to their first church meeting. But nobody showed.

Jack was not discouraged. His experience in Switzerland had tempered his aggressive evangelistic plan. He realized that what looked good on paper didn't always translate in the real world. God was gently molding the dream that he started off with—to evangelize all of Europe in his lifetime. At this point, he had decided he would settle for all of France.

Back to the drawing board, the Joneses and the Wilsons decided to put into practice the mailbox-stuffing technique they had learned from Steve Mullberry in Geneva. Jack and Ben drew up their first *Église du Christ* flyer. Marcie volunteered to watch little Debbie Wilson along with her two children on the following Saturday. The two interns, Kathy and Alice, arrived just in time to pitch in on the work.

---

Saturday arrived with grey clouds spitting rain. Jack, Ben, Amy, Kathy, and Alice met up wearing raincoats at the #23 bus stop on Jack's side of town, in St. Herblain, one of Nantes's suburbs. Ben and Amy were a logical twosome, and Jack bravely took on the rookies. They divided up the surrounding neighborhoods, assigning to each group one rather large subdivision complete with both houses and apartments. Their job was to put one flyer in each mailbox.

Jack took Kathy and Alice to his neighborhood first. Logically, he had thought, he would assign himself to his own immediate surroundings, hoping to meet some of his neighbors. Close to the bus stop where they were starting off, there was an apartment building.

"Let's get this out of the way first," he announced. "Apartment buildings are easy."

The mailboxes were stacked in a giant cube on the bottom level of the building. Jack was sure he could stuff fifty boxes in a matter of minutes. He began by showing Kathy and Alice the proper flyer stuffing technique. "Make sure that you avoid any boxes that have a *publicité interdite* (forbidden to advertise) sticker on them," he added.

As he was telling them that he would go to the adjacent building while they tackled this one on their own, a handsome young man looking to be in his early twenties stepped out of the elevator. Alice, the more social of the two but not the most fluent French speaker by any stretch, couldn't resist a casual *"bonjour"* that dripped with American innocence and a little too much friendliness for Jack's comfort. Though Alice was not trying to flirt, any red-blooded Frenchman would have been crazy not to give her a second glance. She had the features that fit the French stereotype of a young American girl: blonde-hair, blue-eyes, pretty face, slim figure, and a look that screamed she didn't have a clue.

Jack sized the situation up immediately and spoke up in French: "Sir, we are a church group placing some flyers in some boxes today." Then remembering his purpose, he softened: "We would love to have you come and visit us anytime." He extended a sample to the young man. "Please, take one."

*"Merci,"* the young man said. Seeing the more mature, perhaps less clueless-looking and slightly older American man coming to foil his plans, the suave Frenchman moved reluctantly toward the exit.

Jack wiped the sweat off of his brow as he resumed his earlier instruction. "Just stuff the mailboxes in this lobby, and I'll meet you out front when you're done. I'm going to go to the next building over."

About fifteen minutes later, after he completed his box stuffing in the lobby of the building to which he had assigned himself, he opened the glass door and stepped outside, expecting to see the girls walking his direction. He was surprised they had not already entered his building. After all, he was doing the same job both of them were doing together in the neighboring building. When he didn't see them on the sidewalk, he started thinking maybe they were just slow. In that moment, he felt the energy being drained out of him. *Why did God have to send me these two? How in the world are we ever going to get people to come to church at this rate?*

Trying not to let his thoughts catch him in a downward spiral, he quickened his step toward the first building. Upon opening the door, he found he had kept his chin up in vain. He had just enough time to catch a glimpse of the two interns inside the elevator with the same young Frenchman from twenty minutes prior. After the elevator doors closed, all he heard was Alice's voice exclaiming, "Oh, goodness, here we are in the elevator together, and we can't even speak the same language!"

Jack's stomach gave a lurch. He had no way of knowing which floor they were heading toward. He racked his brain, trying to decide whether to follow them up in the next elevator and guess at which floor to get off, whether to take the stairs and try to listen for Alice or Kathy's voices, or whether to just stay where he was and wait for them to come back down. Surely they wouldn't go into a stranger's apartment. He couldn't allow that to happen. He quickly opted for the stairs.

Immediately he prayed for God's protection for the two young girls. Beginning to sweat from the stress again, he reached the first floor and heard Alice laughing. He slowed his run to a walk as he approached the source of the laughter. A door was ajar, and to his horror, while Kathy was laughing, Alice was enunciating in English, loud and clear, "I love you! I love you!"

*What in the world!* Jack thought. He rushed in, grabbed Alice by the arm, and offering no explanation to the young man other than the fact that they had to leave, ushered both ladies out of the building as quickly as possible.

53

Alice seemed sheepish. Kathy spoke up as soon as they were a safe distance from the apartment buildings. "Jack, Alice was just trying to talk to Paul about Jesus. I know what you heard sounded bad, but she didn't mean it in the way you think she did."

Jack grimaced, and Kathy continued her defense.

"The Frenchman we met earlier came back after you left the building. Alice started off by trying to tell him about our church again. Neither one of us could remember the address, so he invited us up to his apartment to look it up in the local directory. As I was about to look in the directory, Alice looked at Paul and said that Jesus loved him very much and that we loved him too. He didn't seem to understand what she was saying, so she just started saying, 'I love you.' I think she was just hoping he would understand what that meant and that she could then explain …"

"Okay, okay," Jack said, interrupting the crazy story. "It's all right. But from now on, don't go into a single man's apartment, okay?"

"Okay," Alice mumbled, deflated.

The rest of the day was mostly uneventful, except for a brief encounter with a young man who spoke English with a perfect British accent and was mildly interested in the flyer. He happened to be returning home as Jack inserted one into his mailbox, and he couldn't help but inquire about what the three Americans were doing in his apartment building. Jack was always grateful for a chance to speak with someone face to face, and this young man seemed particularly interesting. In Jack's mind, he embodied the image of the typical Frenchman, but he was British. They continued their conversation in English. The more he spoke with the man, the more intrigued Jack became. There was something unique about him. Surely this meeting was no accident. They said their good-byes, and Jack walked to the next mailbox, hoping that he and the young man might cross paths again.

When both teams of mailbox stuffers finished their assignments, they all retired to Jack and Marcie's home for a simple sandwich supper. Everyone went to bed early. Sunday would come soon enough.

As he dozed off to sleep, Jack wondered about their day's efforts. *Would anyone take a second look at the "Église du Christ" flyer sitting in those mailboxes that night?*

54

# CHAPTER 8

Sunday arrived, rainy and cold once again. Marcie lay awake, listening to the pitter-pattering noises on the rooftop in the early morning hours while the house was still quiet, wondering if the sun would ever appear in this dreary city. Nantes was gray. And it wasn't just the weather. People appeared even more depressed here than they had in Geneva. *Is it the lack of sunshine that is robbing me of my joy?* she wondered.

She had been finding it more and more difficult to keep the doldrums at bay this season. Life in this place was not how she had envisioned the mission field. It didn't feel as adventurous as she had pictured it. A certain everydayness had overtaken her and depressed her at times. Her urge to vomit didn't help. Fully awake now, she knew she must get something to eat to ease her queasy stomach. Slipping out of bed quietly, she made her way downstairs to the kitchen. There, snacking on a cracker and sipping some ginger tea, she asked God for strength and for Him to send them the lost French sheep.

The next hour was a whir of activity. She tried her best to suppress her gag reflex as she readied herself for church. She brushed MaryAnna's hair and fixed it with a barrette, then dressed wiggly Isaac and threw a few coloring books and crayons into a bag. Jack was busy collecting his thoughts and going over his notes one more time in his head. He rehearsed his sermon mentally as he tied Isaac's shoes, picked him up, and put him in the back seat of the *Deux Chevaux*, for which they had traded the dying Fiat recently.

The Joneses were the first to arrive at the *salle*. Ben, Amy, and little Debbie arrived soon thereafter, with Kathy and Alice not far behind. Amy started the coffee pot, and Ben put a small pamphlet of song sheets on fifteen of the chairs. The children were already running around in circles, so Marcie reeled them in with the coloring books and crayons. Just as Isaac was ripping MaryAnna's Strawberry Shortcake picture in two, someone walked in the door. It was a lady who appeared to be in her fifties. She wore a smile, which was enough to encourage the small group of pioneers. Marcie whispered a threat in English under her breath to Isaac while maintaining perfect outward composure. *Bilingualism has its advantages,* she thought.

The six anxious missionaries had to refrain from falling on the visitor like wolves on their prey. They were thrilled to have a newcomer but didn't want to turn her off by being overly enthusiastic. Her name, she told them, was Jeanine. To their joy, she said she had received the flyer in her mailbox. She was a widow. She had worked as a *crêperie* chef for most of her adult life but was now unemployed. Her only son was married, and she was expecting her first grandson within a few months.

The American group could not have been happier. Seeing that it was time for church service to begin and that she was their only newcomer for the morning, they began with a prayer, a few songs, and then Jack spoke. His lesson was on faith. "Faith," he said, "is believing in something that you cannot see." Jeanine was very responsive to the message. In fact, afterward they all noticed that she enjoyed talking very, very much, probably too much. But they were extremely grateful that God had brought her to them, quirks and all. *If we can't handle annoying personalities, we should never have become missionaries,* Jack reflected.

Jeanine came again the next week, and the next. The team began to study the Bible with her during the week as well. She was curious, open, and eager to grow close to God. The God from the Catholic faith she grew up with looked much different than the one Jack and Ben talked about. She wanted to know more about this One very much indeed.

Ben and Amy were blessed with the gift of inviting. They made a point to invite at least one new person every week. And though most people did not come, one or two did. Within a couple of months, the small group of seekers, including the missionaries, had grown to eleven. It was a very small gathering, but it was a beginning point for the church.

---

One morning Jack woke up early, so he decided to go to the office to pray and study before Ben arrived. He enjoyed the stillness of the drafty *salle*. It was quiet there. He could focus on what was going on with their work, where God was leading them, and what lesson needed to be presented next. He would pull out the commentaries that he had acquired at Harding and prepare for his next lesson. He and Ben took turns preaching and leading singing.

Jack had been brainstorming as to what step they might take next as a church. He was thankful for the few members they had but constantly felt the pressure to bring more in. He decided to start typing the monthly report for supporting churches back home in the States. *Wouldn't it be great if I could report that we are baptizing ten people a month?* he mused. *If an elder came to visit us right now, what would he think of the tiny group we are working with? Surely the group could double in a couple of months.*

Identifying the selfish ambition inside his thoughts, Jack immediately refocused on the work God had set before him to do. He knew outward results were not what impressed God. Nevertheless, he still felt God was going to do something great with them in Nantes, whatever *great* meant. After all, their calling to this city had been crystal clear. Faced with the reality of small numbers, that memory brought him great comfort.

Soon after Jack's arrival, Ben opened the *salle* door and walked upstairs to Jack's office.

"Jack, we have to talk," he said. "I have an idea I want to run by you." He sat in a chair in front of Jack's desk in the small office space. Jack listened, intrigued.

"We need to do a seminar to give the church a jumpstart. You know how Jeanine is always saying that people are not comfortable in their own skin, *"pas bien dans sa peau"*?

"Yes, I've heard her say that a few times."

"Do you remember that seminar that Landon did in St. Louis before we left for Europe? He used a picture of a fish out of water. He told the story of 'Fred the Fish.'"

"Yes! I remember that. Fred the fish is lying on the beach, out of the water. Some guy walks by and says, 'Hey, Fred, how are you today?' and Fred the fish says, 'I think I'm dying' and the guy says, 'Hey, why don't you let me put you back in the water?'"

"That's the one!" Ben said. "And remember in the story, Fred doesn't want to get back into the water? He names all of these things that might help him feel better: a girlfriend, friends, TV, a bigger house. Long story short, of course, none of those things will ever help Fred. The only thing that Fred needs is to be put back into the ocean. But poor Fred can't seem to see the truth."

Jack listened as Ben continued.

"Do you remember what Landon said at the end of the story?"

"Go on."

"Landon said, 'What if there was an element for human beings? What if, like Fred the fish, we are out of our element? I am here to tell you about the element God has for you.'"

Jack lit up. "That was amazing! I remember it now."

"I'm not done," Ben said. "I think that we can hold a seminar right here about Fred the fish and call him *Pierrot le poisson*. I think that on the front of the seminar flyer, we can place our own title, *Bien dans sa peau*, the saying that Jeanine uses all of the time that means 'comfortable in one's own skin.' Don't you think the French might be able to relate to that?"

Jack lost himself in the thought. *Je ne suis pas bien dans ma peau* (I am not comfortable in my skin). *That's it!* Sermon ideas popped into his head left and right, and he mulled over the possibilities: fishing for men, the stream of life found in Jesus, trying to live in a world where we don't belong. It was perfect.

"Thank God, and bravo, Ben!" he exclaimed.

By the end of the day, the two of them had drawn up a rough sketch for the flyer. Very quickly they realized they needed help. Jack called his supporting church in St. Louis. McAlister Road already had a group of students with passports ready to go on a campaign during their spring break holiday but had not decided on the exact location yet. The church agreed to send ten of them to Nantes in about six weeks. Marcie talked to her father on the phone, and he said he wanted to come visit and help them out as well. Having been a preacher most of his life, he had a heart for missions too and wanted to become as involved as he could. Marcie's mother and younger brother and sister even agreed to come.

Jack and Ben were very busy for the next month and a half. Excitement was building within the small team. Ben had an artist from Geneva draw up the illustrations. They advertised on thirty billboards across the city. They bought a printing press, and with the help of Alice and Kathy, they printed and folded 100,000 flyers. They rented the biggest seminar room available, in the *Centre Neptune* building in downtown Nantes, for the occasion. Jack even talked to his father, James Jones, who had worked for a radio station for many years and for the music department at Harding University in the recording studio. His father talked him through how to build electrical boxes for headsets. Jack knew the headsets would be needed for the English-only speakers during the seminar. Jack was planning to translate for Ben, who would be speaking in French. This way, the Americans could listen to the speeches as well.

Marcie was elated when her family arrived, and she welcomed all of the others who came from the States. With the extra hands, the 100,000 flyers were passed out within a week's time. A couple of days before the seminar start date, the team declared a rest day. Marcie's father, however, refused to rest and chose a neighborhood that had not yet been targeted. Thanks to his efforts, at least one couple from that neighborhood decided to attend.

---

The chosen weekend arrived. Amy and Marcie had prepared classes for the children. Ben was ready with his messages. The seminar opened on the first day of spring, in late March. One hundred and ten French people attended the first meeting at *Centre Neptune*. On the second night, when attendance remained high, several French men stood around afterward, talking about the Americans and trying to figure out the meaning of what they were doing. The message the Joneses and Wilsons were sending felt very strange to them. It seemed too good to be true. They were not familiar with it. Even though they were curious, it made them feel uncomfortable.

"There is something not right about this," said Bernard, the man who came as a result of Marcie's father's efforts to distribute flyers on the team's "day of rest."

"Yes, I agree," another man chimed in. "But there certainly doesn't seem to be anything wrong with what they are doing. Something about what they say feels true. But I'm not buying it. Not yet."

"Well, if you ask me," Bernard responded, "there's got to be something or someone behind all of this. Maybe it has to do with money. There's a catch. Why would a group want to just reach out and bring a message like this to perfect strangers and not expect anything in return?"

Jack overheard the conversation, and his throat became dry. He gathered his wits and walked up boldly to the group of men.

"I can answer your questions," he said.

Immediately fifteen heads turned and looked at him expectantly. Jack felt like Daniel in the lions' den: He was fresh meat surrounded by wild animals ready to pounce.

"So, what's the name? What do you call yourselves? What or who is behind this?" Bernard prodded brazenly.

"I could give you a name," Jack spoke evenly, "but if I gave you a short answer, you might go home and look it up, and it might not make sense to you. The only way you can know who we are is by getting to know us. Give us a chance. Let us show you instead of telling you."

"That's fair," Bernard responded, satisfied. Jack breathed a sigh of relief.

Throughout the seminar, God brought in people who were eager to study the Bible. After the weekend came to a close, the team formed three groups of newcomers to meet for the purpose of studying the Bible for twelve weeks. The *Église du Christ* in Nantes enjoyed forty extra people in its services. Eventually half drifted away, but twenty, including Bernard and his wife, Elise, stayed and became members. They learned to trust the group of Americans, but most of all, they developed a relationship with Jesus Christ for the first time.

---

The first signs of spring finally began to appear, and for Marcie it was a turning point. Jonquils were poking their heads timidly up out of the ground. Marcie discovered a bird's nest in one of the trees behind the house. From March through May, something new would appear weekly: tulips, bright with their yellows, pinks, purples, and reds; then daffodils and Easter lilies. Winter was gone at last. Although Marcie knew that her nausea would not abate until late May, seeing new life rise up from the ground reminded her that she would soon see the new life growing inside her womb.

When May came in all its glory, Jack took a day off so his family could visit the *Jardin des Plantes*, a botanical garden located close to the train station in Nantes. It was breathtaking. Chrysanthemums, roses, camellias, daisies, tulips, and violets lined the pathways. Wildflowers filled empty, wintry spaces with simple beauty. There were bluebells, pimpernels, bugles, bellflowers, poppies, buttercups, forget-me-nots, goldenrods, lily of the valley, and marigolds.

In spite of Marcie's earlier doldrums, she and Jack agreed they truly were living the dream: working on the mission field together, watching the church grow beautifully like the blossoms around them, and experiencing parenthood. As she thought of the third child inside, Marcie smiled. *My cup runs over with blessings.*

———————

A few weeks after the family's *Jardin des Plantes* excursion, Marcie awoke one morning to "winteresque" temperatures despite the spring season. Chilly springtime days like this one brought back memories of the long, drab winter. Even though June was only a week away, the sun refused to shine, and the afternoon temperature was only fifty degrees. The locals said, *"Il fait Nantes,"* meaning the weather was "Nantes-ish." Marcie was determined to get out anyway. She invited Amy to meet her at a nearby park so the kids could play together. Marcie and Amy, it seemed, ran hot and cold in their friendship. Though they got along well when it came to the team, they hadn't formed a strong bond outside of church work. Neither one wanted to force the issue, and both understood each other's boundaries. However, they also knew that their children needed each other's company occasionally, so they tried to put forth some effort for them.

Marcie put Isaac in the stroller and readjusted his toddler hat. Thankfully it was fastened underneath his chin, as he tugged at it constantly in an effort to remove it.

"MaryAnna! Get your coat on. It's time to go!" she called to her five-year-old as she grabbed her own coat and bundled up. She locked the door behind them.

As she walked out of the neighborhood, Marcie began feeling sorry for herself. She sometimes missed her teaching days at West Memphis Christian School. Although she had always wanted to become a missionary and a mother, she missed the career that she'd had in the States, the steadiness of schedules, the classroom full of children, the pedagogy. Perhaps it was just the drudgery of everyday life. *I would probably have dreary days as a teacher too,* she reasoned, but more thoughts crowded in to worry her. Jack had been away from home several evenings in a row, studying for sermon material. Although she understood that he needed a quiet place to read, she missed his presence in the evenings. But she was also determined to remain strong and supportive. A little fresh air and exercise would be just the thing to take her mind off her increasingly absent husband and to brighten up the children's day.

She pushed Isaac's stroller briskly on the sidewalk, and MaryAnna skipped along beside. Her bulging belly bumped into the stroller whenever she tilted it to go up a curb. When the three of them arrived at the park, Amy and six-year-old Debbie were already there. Debbie was on the monkey bars, dangling upside down and waving at MaryAnna to come and join her. Amy was sitting on a bench. She smiled and waved. Marcie pushed the stroller over to her as MaryAnna skipped off to join her playmate.

As the mothers watched their girls, Marcie gave Isaac his morning snack of dry cereal in a cup. Amy snacked on some trail mix in a plastic container.

"Hungry?" Amy asked and extended her bowl toward Marcie as an offering.

Marcie politely refused. She was not very fond of Amy's concoctions. They usually consisted of at least five different types of nuts with an assortment of dried fruits and veggies—sometimes even a few black olives. The combinations were a little too strange for Marcie, who had developed a new aversion to nuts during this pregnancy.

Amy jumped right into church talk, their most natural conversation topic.

"I was so excited to see the *Fusil* and the *Rondeau* families again last Sunday!"

"Me too," Marcie agreed. "That seminar was the best thing that has happened to our *Église du Christ* since we've been here."

"I hope Jeanine is doing better. Didn't she say that she had bronchitis again?"

"Oh dear, you're right. I forgot about that. Do you think we should bring her a meal?"

"Probably. I'll do my chicken casserole if you want."

"Ok, great! I'll do vegetables and dessert."

Eventually the church small talk was exhausted. As they were about to broach another subject, Marcie looked up just in time to see Debbie running away from MaryAnna, the former laughing hysterically and MaryAnna looking quite unhappy in comparison. MaryAnna ran to her mom and complained that Debbie had called her a name. Marcie, uncomfortable in front of Amy and not sure what to do, simply urged MaryAnna to play on the slides or to try the swings instead. Amy ignored the whole incident.

Miffed, Marcie tried to continue the conversation. Her feathers were ruffled, however, and she was growing weary of trying to figure out how to handle these awkward scenarios, which continued to occur against her hopes. Having felt the call to the mission field right along with Jack, Marcie nevertheless knew her number one mission field was her family, and she desired to keep her "chicks" gathered under her wing. Indeed, she took great stock in raising her children in the ways she thought were right. Amy's parenting approach troubled Marcie greatly, and her sense of justice had just been disturbed.

Sensing the tension, the women switched their conversation topic to school, when they would enroll their daughters and their hope for good teachers. As they began sharing what they knew about the schools, Marcie saw Debbie hit MaryAnna. She didn't think Amy saw it, but presently Amy got up and walked over to her daughter. "Deborah Kate Wilson, you know you shouldn't hit people," she said. "Do you think you could tell MaryAnna you are sorry?"

Apparently Debbie didn't feel much like apologizing, so off she trotted to the sandbox. Amy said nothing more and returned to the bench.

Marcie knew that as teammates, she and Amy were supposed to get along, so she was at a loss as to what to do. She felt her "mama bear claws" starting to come out in defense of her daughter, overpowering a reasonable response. But she could see nothing good coming out of confronting Amy. *What if Amy became resentful? What would the church members think if they knew that there was a chink in the team armor?* No, Amy's weakness as a parent in Marcie's eyes would be better kept hidden even though the ongoing conflict of parenting styles was a big source of discouragement for Marcie. She found it difficult to want to be with Amy, and yet she felt that she must. She was reaching her wit's end. She told herself she would not initiate a get-together again for a long time.

After seeing there was no apparent wound, Marcie tried to distract her daughter. "MaryAnna, see if Debbie wants to play on the slide." Then she turned her attention to Amy, attempting to steer the conversation to a more friendly subject once more.

"I think the interns are doing really well, don't you? They seem to have adjusted to their lives in France."

"Yes," Amy responded. "I think Alice especially has embraced the French. Do you remember the story Jack told us about her stuffing the mailboxes and accidentally declaring her love to that Frenchman?"

They both laughed at the memory and shared stories about their own latest cultural blunders. Amy then asked Marcie how she was feeling about becoming a mother of three. Just when Marcie was feeling her coldness toward Amy begin to thaw, Debbie stomped over to her mother.

"It's time to go, Mommy!" she declared.

"Okay, sweetie. Just a few more minutes, and then we'll leave," Amy said, attempting to put her off.

Debbie threw herself on the ground in protest. "*Moh-mmmeee! I* want to go home and play Barbies! I *neeeeeed* to play with them! We have to go *now!*"

Amy was visibly embarrassed. "Oh well. I guess I don't have a choice!" she said sheepishly to Marcie.

Marcie's spunk and mouth had gotten her into trouble many a time. The problem was, choice words popped into her brain so quickly, and it was difficult to resist the temptation to let them set sail with pleasure across her tongue. There was something almost physically satisfying about putting someone in her place. Unfortunately, even though such an endeavor usually ended in Marcie apologizing, there was a short in the circuit if Marcie was angry enough. So in the moment, she succumbed to her inner urging, ignoring all warning flags.

"Yes, Amy, you *do* have a choice. If only you could put as much energy into raising Debbie as you put into other things like saving ice cubes and making granola, then maybe MaryAnna could have a decent playmate."

The sting was great. Amy quietly put the top back onto the plastic container of granola snack. She rose from the bench, took Debbie's hand, and walked back down the path toward the bus stop

64

from which they had come, all without a single word of response or a good-bye.

Marcie was incredulous. *What just happened? Did I really let out such biting words?* Still hot from exploding with such venom, she was already beginning to feel the molten lava of guilt harden into black rock inside.

*Surely there is no hope for the friendship to continue now. And what will I tell Jack?* A wave of dread settled in on her at the thought of what Jack would say. She would have to tell him. She would not be able to blame this one on "pregnancy hormones." She and Jack and Amy and Ben would probably have to meet as couples to resolve the matter. She would have to apologize even though she felt in the bottom of her soul that she was right. *Oh, if only I had just held my tongue!*

All the way home, Marcie's thoughts frantically replayed the scene. One voice told her Amy deserved what she got, that her anger had been festering long enough. But she knew that was the wrong voice to heed. Even if Amy deserved a small portion of what she had said, the approach was wrong. There was a time and place to rebuke someone, and at the park in the heat of the moment was not that time or place. She did her best to watch for cars as she navigated the stroller and MaryAnna across the street, holding MaryAnna's hand firmly to be sure that nothing else disastrous happened on their way back to the house. As she did so, she felt as though her world was crumbling around her. Her thoughts kept coming back to how she was going to explain everything to Jack.

Once at home, she fixed a quick lunch for her children and found she could not consume much more than a nibble. She felt nauseous, and this time it was not due to morning sickness. She put Isaac down for a nap and let MaryAnna color for a while. And then she debated about whether or not to call Amy. If she did, what would she say? She wondered what Amy was thinking and if there was any chance of reconciliation. *Oh, how will I ever make it through the afternoon until Jack comes home?*

# CHAPTER 9

Jack locked up the *salle* and sat down at the wheel of the *Deux Chevaux*. On his way home, he reflected on the work he'd accomplished during the day: meeting with one of the newest members of the church, studying the Bible, hashing out sermon topics with Ben for the next three months, and finally starting on his next Sunday morning lesson. Since it was Friday, however, he was feeling the pressure to finish preparing for the church time sermon. Perhaps Marcie would understand if he had to spend the evening studying so he could spend all of Saturday with the family.

It seemed like there was never enough time to study. Most of his commutes back home involved at least some degree of wondering where the day had gone. During work hours, someone always interrupted what he was doing. He was going to have to find a place to study other than the *salle*. Ben was also a constant, hovering presence. It wasn't that he disliked him in the least, but Ben was quick to ask him for help and advice about a lesson here and there. Jack needed more uninterrupted study time. *Maybe next week will be better,* he thought. *In the meantime, I'll have to do the best I can and hope Marcie will extend some grace to me tonight.*

When he pulled up to the house and turned off the car, he felt a strange storm cloud brewing. He looked in the window at the yellow light coming from the house. One of the children was crying, and Marcie was obviously instructing him or her about something. *Oh boy*, he thought. He opened the door to spilled milk on the carpet in the living room, MaryAnna crying, Isaac laughing, and Marcie looking at him with a strange mixture of weariness and he wasn't sure what else. He scooped up MaryAnna and gave Marcie a kiss.

The family sat down to a dinner of noodles and tomato sauce with green beans on the side. Although it was a favorite with MaryAnna and Isaac, he was not fond of this particular menu and Marcie knew it. It was rare for him to comment negatively on food of any sort, particularly a meal cooked by his beloved Marcie. One evening he'd mustered up all of his courage to let her know that a plate of plain noodles covered with tomato sauce straight from a can was not very enjoyable to him. He remembered the moment well.

*Something must have happened today to make Marcie resort to this less-than-par, last-minute dish,* he thought. Deciding it must have been a rough day for Marcie and that he had better not add to its misery, especially since he was hoping for a favor from her after dinner, he determined it would be better to eat the noodles and canned tomato sauce without comment. He offered to do the dishes when the meal was finished.

Marcie was unusually silent. After the meal, she wiped off the children's faces methodically and took them upstairs to give them a bath. As Jack washed and rinsed the four dinner plates and placed them in the drying rack, he began rehearsing how he would break the news to her about needing just a little more time to study. At times like this one, he felt trapped between his desire to please Marcie and his determination to be the best missionary preacher he could possibly be. God had called him to this job, and he wanted to work at it with all of his heart! *Marcie will understand. Well, she should anyway.* He thought he might try to buffer the blow by suggesting some family time tomorrow. Maybe he could even offer to let her go to a shop or two by herself! That would surely buy him some study time tonight, he reasoned.

Marcie dressed the children for bed and read them their nightly Bible story. She sang them a song, as she did every night, and then closed the door gently. How was she going to tell Jack about what happened today? As dreadful as the pit of her stomach felt, she knew she had to talk to him as soon as possible. Her weakness of speaking too quickly had a mirroring quality: she never let things fester for long. She tiptoed down the stairs to Jack drying off his hands and placing the towel back on the oven handle, turned into the family room, and sat down on the couch, expecting Jack to join her so that they could finally talk.

Jack walked in but remained standing.

"Marcie, thank you for being such a supportive wife," he said, clearing his throat a bit self-consciously. "I hope you know what a tremendous role you play in our mission work here by supporting me and allowing me to do the work I need to do."

Ordinarily Marcie would have seen exactly where he was going with this comment. But her mind was so completely overtaken with the weight of her guilt that she heaped even more condemnation on herself, believing that she deserved no such compliment!

"I really want to make sure that I'm home more on Friday nights. But tonight I have a few more things to finish up."

Marcie made no response. He suddenly felt like his speech was losing its potency and found himself floundering for excuses.

"Ben spent at least an hour this morning talking to me about a new idea he has for our Sunday school class. Jeanine called to tell me she'd read the whole New Testament. She was so excited about it that she talked for at least twenty minutes, and I didn't feel like I could cut her off." He was about to add that he was also having trouble with his sinuses and had to drop by the pharmacy to pick up some medicine to relieve his symptoms, but he was cut short by the look on her face.

Practically bursting with what had become like a small bombshell inside of her, Marcie showed signs of panic in her eyes. Her mind whirled. *He still has his shoes on. He is about to walk out that door, and knowing him, he won't be back until eleven o'clock! And I am too tired to wait that long to talk to him.* Other realities suddenly came crashing in on her. *He has left the house in the evening every night this week! How can he keep doing this! I need him to be my husband sometimes and not just "Jacques the preacher"!*

The frustration and drama from the day turned into anger again. None of it would have happened if Amy had the guts to stand up to her own child. And maybe if Jack had stayed home at least one night this week, she might not have been so frazzled and spewed hurtful words at Amy in the first place!

"Jack, you have left the house every night this week to go study. When are you going to put the family first?"

He was not prepared for her comment.

"I don't leave every night. You are exaggerating. Look, I know you have had a long day. I'm going to make it up to you. Would you like to do some shopping tomorrow? I will watch the kids. You can go by yourself! Or you could ask Amy if she wants to come along."

"Ha! Amy, huh? What a great idea!" she said, her voice dripping with sarcasm.

Jack didn't like the way the conversation was going. He was the head of the household, after all. Marcie should be a little more submissive in situations such as these. She should learn to trust him more. She should know that he always had the family's best interest in mind.

"Marcie, I'm sorry you feel this way. Maybe the timing is not great, but I really have to get a few more things finished. I'll try to hurry. We can talk about it more later. I'm just going to find a coffee shop where I can go and be alone. I'm sure I can get a lot accomplished. I'll try to be back in an hour and a half, okay?"

Marcie's feelings of condemnation returned. She didn't really deserve for him to stay and talk to her anyway, not after what she had done today. "Okay," she mumbled."

She heard the engine turn over twice before it actually started. *And there's another thing,* she thought. *We are going to have to get the car fixed.* It felt to her like there was always something else needing to be fixed that they couldn't quite afford. Their car was barely making it most mornings. Jack had even had to push it down the hill on their street one day to get it going. But that was the least of her worries now. She was stuck at home with the weight of her guilt and no one to help her relieve it. Not even Jack, her best friend!

*Who can I turn to?* she wondered. Her mother was a long-distance call away—something she and Jack could only afford for special occasions or emergencies. *Well, perhaps this is an emergency. . . . No.* She refused to heap more guilt on herself by incurring a high telephone expense. But there was certainly nobody here that she could talk to. Ben and Amy were out of the question.

Her thoughts suddenly began to wrap themselves around the possible conversation that Ben and Amy were having right now. Oh, she was so miserable! She wanted more than anything to be a good Christian woman, but she felt tortured by her mistake and so very alone. Sentiments of martyrdom began to sink in. She had followed her husband across the ocean to a foreign land. As it turned out, her role was mainly domestic. And now, to add to her sad state, she was left to bear her situation alone. She felt sorry for herself because of her current predicament. Indeed, living in France was miserable, and especially so when the weather was so cold and dreary, as it had been today.

Thoughts of the calling God had on her life and the small, growing church were not enough to cheer her this time. A lump developed in her throat. She fought the urge to cry and then realized suddenly there was no sense in resisting. No one was around to hear her, to see her eyes become puffy and red, or to notice her mascara running down her face. The children were asleep and the house was still. She let the sobs come out slowly and quietly at first, and then, with shaking shoulders, cried quite pitifully for a good five minutes. *Enough,* she told herself at last and went to the bathroom to wipe her nose.

As she flopped back down on the couch and reached for the afghan, she felt a familiar voice say, "I'm here."

Instinctively she picked up her Bible and remembered that her best friend had been here with her all along. *Oh God, thank you for reminding me You are here. Please help me! I feel so lonely. I wish I could see You, talk to You face to face. I need a friend, and I know that You are my friend, so I am not alone. Will you please help me to feel Your presence more? And will You please send me someone I can talk to here?*

The next sound she heard was a car's engine sputter and then shut off. The car's door squeaked open and then slammed shut. *He's home.*

---

It had taken Jack just ten minutes to arrive at his coffee shop destination. As soon as he arrived and ordered his usual *café noir,* he took his journal out of his briefcase to make a note about the time. Journaling was his way of keeping himself accountable, and he was meticulous about it. Soon after his career as a missionary had begun, he was convicted about keeping a record of his activities. He'd been privy to too many friends' careers plummeting due to a common elder board question in the form of the famous complaint, "What do you do all day?" Jack was determined to be prepared with a record of activities should he be asked to give a detailed report. He'd never imagined using his journal in a situation such as the one he was facing now.

"You leave the house every night to go study." He could hear Marcie's accusing voice in his head. He opened his notebook, intending to prove himself right in the argument. *I can show her that I've been at home quite frequently these past few weeks,* he reasoned. He opened the journal to his entry from two weeks prior.

*Monday, May 2, 1980*

*9:00. Visited with Jeanine and her neighbor in the morning over coffee. Reviewed Sunday morning's lesson together and answered several questions that her neighbor had about church. Ben couldn't come. He was ill. Returned three phone calls before lunch. Brief lunch with the interns.*

*12:30 to 2:00. Studied until someone called the church office by mistake. It was a wrong number, but the person started asking questions. Turned into a long conversation about the end of the world. Also asked such questions as "Why would you try to do something different than what the Catholics are doing? We are all Catholics here. We don't need any of your American protestant religion."*

*2:40. Resumed studying.*

*2:53. Kathy called to say she had locked her keys in her apartment and could I please come let her in with the spare key.*

He paused to reflect on that last entry. Thankfully he'd had the idea that either Ben or he should have a backup key in case such an emergency should arise. He congratulated himself again mentally at having foreseen the need. Annoyed that Alice inexplicably had been unavailable that day, he'd made the 10-minute commute over to Kathy's apartment to let her in. By the time he returned to the office, it was 3:40. Feeling his stress level rise, he skipped to the end of that day's entry.

*7:30. After dinner, returned to the office for two hours to finish studying.*

Okay, he thought, *so I went back out to study that evening. That was two weeks ago.* He turned the page to what he'd written the next day.

*Tuesday, May 3, 1980*

*8:30 to 9:00. Prayed with Ben at the office.*

71

*9:00 to 10:00. Talked with Ben about the Bible study this evening. Ben is supposed to teach this time. He wanted feedback on his ideas. He has decided to begin a study on Galatians.*

*10:10. Interns arrived and started on their daily office tasks. Talked to Kathy about answering the phone, talked to Alice about sorting and filing some church paper work and bank statements, etc.*

*11:00 to 11:45. Continued studying for my sermon on Sunday.*

*11:50. Lunch with the team.*


Impatient and eager to get to the evening portion, Jack skipped to the end of his entry.

*7:15. Studied at Café au Coin until 9:00 p.m.*


*Huh. Two days in a row I was not at home in the evening,* he admitted to himself. He continued to read. The following three days in his journal ended in the same way: studying for about two hours or more every night away from home. He was incredulous. But his journal wouldn't lie to him. He continued reading. Saturday: same. Sunday, yes, even Sunday after he preached! He remembered that he had thought maybe, if he could get a head start on the week with studying, then he wouldn't have to go out in the evenings so much.

He turned another page to see the expected improvement. Monday evening: more studying. Tuesday evening: more studying. Finally he closed his journal. It was true. Marcie had been right. He regretted the words he'd spoken to her earlier. He could hardly believe he had allowed himself to become so deceived. Leaving his coffee cup unfinished, he rose to leave. The waiter came to collect his cup and raised his French eyebrows at the remaining contents.

"*Ça ne va pas, Monsieur?*" ("Are you not well, sir?")

Jack assured the man he was fine. Although he had only been in Nantes three months, the staff at *Café au Coin* already knew that leaving anything in a cup was definitely not a practice of *Jacques* Jones.

Back in the car, he thanked God for allowing the *Deux Chevaux* to start. On the drive home, he pondered his miscalculation

72

of how he'd been spending his time. How easy it was for him to get so completely caught up in ministry that he didn't realize he was neglecting his family. As important as his job was to him, he knew that it should never take the place of his family. He had allowed his priorities to become a little blurry in his own mind. Marcie was so good for him in this regard. She was quick to point out imbalance. He thanked God for her, and he prayed for her during the rest of his drive home.

---

When Jack opened the door to his home a few minutes after 9 o'clock, Marcie was there to greet him. She fell into his arms, and neither spoke. He wrapped his arms around her and began apologizing.

"Marcie, can you forgive me for leaving the house so much? I didn't realize what I was doing. You were right."

He could tell that she had been crying. Her face was smeared with mascara. But she seemed more peaceful than before he had left. That vibrant spirit he knew underneath the face was shining through.

"Of course I forgive you. I hated to see you walk out, but it turned into something good."

Jack gave her a quizzical look.

"Jack, I wish I had a friend here, someone to have coffee with and just chat with. I wish Amy and I were closer. You're my closest friend, but even you let me down sometimes. This evening after you left, I realized I had been neglecting my very best friend, Jesus. I took some time to pray. And now I need to tell *you* what happened to me today."

She told him everything. She didn't hold back any of the details from the fight with Amy. He didn't interrupt. He just listened. He was surprised and dismayed. So soon after his sincere apology, he was frustrated with Marcie again. He expected Marcie to support the work here in Nantes. The words she'd spoken to Amy could cause a serious rift in the team. *Why could she not control herself?* he thought angrily.

His mental accusations were interrupted by a convicting thought. *"Jack,"* the still, small voice said, *"you have been struggling with self-control too."*

He knew it was true. How many nights in the last few weeks had he justified leaving his family to go study? He'd allowed his job to occupy too lofty a position. It was time for him to remove the "plank from his own eye" and show forgiveness to Marcie for her "speck." Without a word, he took her into his arms and held her for a long time.

Marcie sobbed into Jack's shoulder. It felt so good to be free of her torturous secret. And it felt even better to reconcile with Jack. Together they decided they would set up a time to talk with Ben and Amy as soon as possible. They agreed they didn't want to leave any time for wounds to fester.

First thing in the morning, Jack called the Wilsons and invited them over for a late breakfast. When they arrived, Amy was subdued. She stood for a long time, watching Debbie intently. She forbade Debbie from playing with MaryAnna. Instead, she made sure that Debbie sat quietly and looked at the book she'd brought. Marcie realized Amy's change in behavior was a result of the harsh words she'd said the day before at the park.

Marcie apologized as best as she could. She admitted that her words had been inappropriate. She humbly asked Amy for forgiveness. Amy accepted Marcie's words and warmed up a little. The four of them then had breakfast together and a short time of prayer.

---

During the weeks that followed the incident, Marcie and Amy didn't see much of each other outside of church gatherings or team planning times. On Debbie's seventh birthday though, just before the beginning of summer, Amy invited the Jones family over. MaryAnna and Isaac played well with Debbie, who eagerly showed them her toys and shared very nicely, without a single argument.

Summer arrived with blossoming fruit from apple and cherry trees. The church, too, was flourishing: the congregation grew to forty members. They knew the number might seem small to American Christians, but those who had experienced European mission regarded the number with respect. The newly planted church was putting down roots. The four missionaries and their interns were finding soft spots in the rock hard religious tradition in Western

European countries that blocked the gospel from reaching many of its citizens. They believed earnestly that they would penetrate the cold, hard sod of the hearts of the lost in the city of Nantes, France.

# CHAPTER 10

Jack tried not to stare at the new couple that had just walked into the Sunday morning service one bright morning in June. The man was very good looking, and he carried himself with confidence. He was tall, had light brown hair, and his skin tone was very light as well. He looked athletic and was well dressed with a periwinkle button-up shirt, white slacks, and brown sandals. He had a perfectly symmetrical nose, and as he smiled, he looked out of brown eyes to the eclectic group around him. *He certainly is different*, Jack thought, looking around at the individuals who had ventured through the doors of the *Église Du Christ de Nantes* thus far. It would take him a few minutes to remember where he had seen the man before.

His wife had her hand draped elegantly around his arm. She was every bit as good looking as he was. She had dark hair and dark features with olive-toned skin. Her face was fresh and beautiful. Her brown eyes shone with friendliness and curiosity. Her nose turned up in the cutest button fashion, and she had perfectly shaped lips, which smiled widely. Her hair, long and wavy, fell in heaps over her shoulders and concealed the top of her purse strap. She wore flattering clothes, a long and flowing brown skirt and a white peasant style blouse, very French but not risqué or immodest.

Although the two of them were somewhat intimidating to look at, they immediately put everyone at ease with their warm greeting, introducing themselves as François and Pauline Forrester. It was then that Jack remembered where he had first seen the man. He had stopped Jack in the apartment building to inquire about the flyer placed in his mailbox several months ago during the first mailbox stuffing in the winter, the day of Alice's blunder with the Frenchman.

The morning service went unusually well that day. Afterward, everyone surrounded François and Pauline and enjoyed getting to know them. They both appeared to be in their late twenties or early thirties, like the Wilsons and the Joneses. François easily shared many interesting details about their lives. He said he worked as a manager for *Leclerc,* a large French supermarket. Although he was British, he had met and married Pauline while living in France. His father had fought alongside the French in World War II and had named his son after a French soldier who saved his life. Pauline shared that she was born and raised in France—Nantes, in fact. She taught first grade in a nearby school. Pauline was also fluent in English and spoke it with an adorable French accent. Indeed, with their intriguing mix of French and British accents and knowledge of languages, they made quite a smashing duo.

Marcie was excited to meet someone who was gifted with children. Pauline seemed like an answer to her prayer. It would be so wonderful to have a teacher as a friend, someone trained as she had been at Harding University, the career she had forsaken for mission work. She would welcome some help in the children's ministry area of the church.

Although the fellowship time after church went well, Jack was a bit concerned that the regular attenders might have overwhelmed the Forresters. Nevertheless, they returned the following week and the week after that one. Not long afterward, François met with Jack and Ben privately to discuss his spiritual life with them. He had become a Christian as a child in his parents' church, he said. It was an evangelical church, and he expressed that the *Église du Christ* church service reminded him of the way he had been brought up as a child. He very much wanted to be a part of a church again and put God first in his life. He confessed that he had become distracted with his job and a few worldly temptations that he did not describe, but he longed to straighten his priorities. Jack and Ben were thrilled. They agreed to meet with him once a week to help guide him in Bible study.

François's spiritual growth thereafter was rapid. He had a strong foundation compared to the other attendees, so it did not take long before Jack and Ben regarded him as a potential leader in the church. He was a breath of fresh air for the young team of missionaries.

Pauline hungered to know God better and live out her Christian walk with her brothers and sisters. Although she had been raised Catholic, as most French people were, she had been forced to reexamine her religion when she married François. Her family had threatened to disown her when she became engaged to a Protestant. But her stubborn spirit prompted her to stand by the man she loved. She determined to take her religion into her own hands. She was more curious than ever about the Bible and listened carefully as the Americans enlightened her on passages she never knew existed.

During one of their weekly meetings, François shared with Jack and Ben that he wanted to recommit his life to Christ and be baptized. On the day of the baptism, since the weather was warm, the church met on the shore of the *Erdre*, one of the rivers that ran through Nantes. Ben led the group in singing *"Humilie-toi Devant le Seigneur"* ("Humble Yourself in the Sight of the Lord") and *"Chante Alleluia Au Seigneur"* ("Sing Hallelujah to the Lord") while François and Jack waded into the river together. As the pair reached waist level in the water, Jack put his hand on François's shoulder and turned to the small gathering on the shore. He felt a large lump in his throat. Looking up toward heaven, he sensed God's hand on him as he prepared to help a brother dedicate his life to Christ. Jesus had begun his ministry with baptism. Today marked a new beginning in the life of the *Église du Christ de Nantes.* A thrill filled Jack, and he shivered with joy.

*"Francois, je te baptise au nom du Pére, du Fils, et du Saint Esprit"* ("François, I baptize you in the name of the Father, the Son, and the Holy Spirit").

When François rose up out of the water, cheering and clapping came from those gathered on the shore. A praise song broke out as Amy, Marcie, and Pauline handed towels to François and Jack. New excitement was evident among the small group gathered on the riverbank. Some passers by gawked, laughed, and pointed. But nothing could quench the thrill that the small body of believers felt that day.

François's baptism caused the floodgates to open in the small church. Many more decided to become baptized during the following weeks, including Pauline. Like the farmer sowing his seed in the book of Mathew, Jack and Ben had sown their seed as well, and God was bringing forth a harvest.

# PART III

# Life on the Field

# CHAPTER 11

Marcie screamed in agonizing pain as another contraction gripped her body. The nurse responded by instructing her to push but not to be so loud. *What? She is actually shushing me!* Marcie thought. Anger strengthened her to push all the harder.

"Can you see the head yet?" she asked Jack desperately as the contraction subsided temporarily.

Jack could not see it, so he quickly redirected his answer. "You are doing great! It won't be long now. The baby will be here soon."

*How long? How long!* Marcie thought as a new, stronger wave of searing pain threw her lower abdomen into one huge convulsion. She didn't remember having to work this hard with either MaryAnna or Isaac. *Just get this baby out!* she prayed.

Three long hours of pushing finally exploded into ecstatic relief as the nurse, doctor, and nurse's assistant announced together, *"C'est un garçon!"* ("It's a boy!")

Jack and Marcie basked in the glow of another precious, perfect child. They named him Thomas Cor Jones.

It was October 31, 1980, but not much candy giving or costume wearing would happen on this day because Halloween was not celebrated in France. Jack and Marcie could not have cared less.

Unlike postpartum with Isaac and MaryAnna, which had been relatively easy, this one brought new challenges for Marcie. Thomas's birth took a harsh toll on her body, and it would take months for her to recover fully. The doctors told her to take it easy, to try to find a way to stop going up and down the stairs in her house. Jack stayed home from work for the first week that she was home from the hospital. When he announced that he would return to work the following week, she sobbed. She felt overwhelmed with a four-year-old and a toddler to care for at home besides this precious newborn baby. So Jack stayed with her an extra week to help her to recover and adjust to her newest responsibility.

Finally the time came for Jack to resume his old commute. *At last,* he thought as he sat behind the wheel of his sputtering *Deux Chevaux* on a rainy Monday, driving to the *salle*. The windshield wipers worked furiously to keep the pelting rain off the glass, protecting him from the moisture blasts of the November storm. He

81

felt happy about his growing family and yet exhausted. *Why does so much of parenthood, even the most exciting parts, have to be lived out amid such fatigue and weariness?* he wondered. He had been awakened every night for the past couple of weeks to help Marcie with the precious new life that God had blessed them with, either to change a diaper or to help soothe the newborn back to sleep. *Will I forget about the fatigue after Thomas grows older? I can't believe that I wanted twelve children at one point,* he chuckled to himself.

Despite his blood-shot eyes, weary body, and the downpour on the metal roof of the car, he found solace in going back to work. He loved Marcie deeply for the way she selflessly offered herself to her children, and he could not have been more thankful to be leaving her in charge on the home front. As he drove the familiar route to the *salle,* he marveled at how much time had passed since his family's arrival in Nantes. A year ago at this time, they were living in Geneva and waiting for God's call. Now they were fully settled into a town to which they believed God had specifically called them.

His oldest, MaryAnna, now attended the nearby neighborhood elementary school. His mind flashed back to the adventure he'd had with her on her very first day of school, September 1, just a few months ago.

"Mommy, I don't want to go to school! Please, Mommy, can I stay home with you and Isaac?" MaryAnna pleaded.

Jack took her four-year-old hand, clammy from nervousness, and held it in a firm grip as he opened the front door and said good-bye to Marcie. The two of them walked to *Soleil Levant* together. MaryAnna had always been submissive to her parents and desirous to please them. Jack knew she was dreading this day, so he tried to make small talk about what she might do at her new French school. When she remained pale, he changed the subject altogether and talked about her new baby brother, Thomas Cor. She perked up only a little and commented back briefly. She was ordinarily so happy and often hyper. It saddened him to see her distraught.

Jack did as he always did when he was at a loss: he prayed. MaryAnna couldn't hear him, but he begged God not to leave her side at this school where she was a perfect stranger, where she couldn't even speak the language. After much discussion, he and Marcie had agreed that as long as they lived on this mission field where God had put them, they would not keep their children in a protective shell. God might open more doors for ministry through them, they believed, if they lived like the people around them. MaryAnna gripped his hand more tightly as the school came into view.

Jack glanced down at her. MaryAnna had on her new back-to-school outfit: a knee length, straight, lavender-colored polyester skirt with a matching white and lavender polka dotted blouse with puffed sleeves. Marcie had carefully tucked the shirt in and fastened the shiny purple belt. She had received the clothing in a special package from her own mother for MaryAnna's first day of school. She had pulled MaryAnna's hair back into a ponytail with a purple rubber band. Matching clothes was definitely more of an American custom than a French one, so MaryAnna stood out from the other children arriving at the school. *Lord,* he prayed, *here is our child. I trust You to keep her safe and somehow use her and her school experiences in Your plan to reach the people of France with the gospel. Protect her just like You did when she was so sick in the Geneva hospital years ago.*

Continuing to clutch Jack's hand, she stepped into the school courtyard in her new brown leather shoes with shiny silver buckles, more evidence of Marcie's efforts. A gaggle of other children were gathered with their parents. Some were crying but most were just standing around silently, waiting for their summer vacation to come to a close officially with the sound of the first school bell.

Jack was thankful they had arrived a little early. He noticed a young French girl about MaryAnna's size who was standing in the middle of the playground by herself. She had brown eyes, glasses, and dark hair in a bob haircut—a common hairdo among little French girls. Like MaryAnna, she was dressed in her brand new back-to-school outfit: a light blue button-up blouse and a navy, green, and yellow plaid gingham skirt, pleated at the knees and extending just above her calves. She wore black tights and shiny black Mary Jane style shoes. Her mid-morning snack (*casse-croute*) was in one hand, and with her other hand she was wiping tears from her face.

Though the girl was distressed, Jack could not have been more relieved. One of the greatest comforts to a human heart is another soul in agony. He led MaryAnna over to the child and began to talk to her. "*Bonjour! Ça va?*" ("How are you?") he asked.

The girl blubbered an unintelligible response, so Jack tried to tell her in the best child friendly French he knew that it was normal to be nervous and afraid on the first day of school. Then he told her he thought she was going to have a good teacher and that her day would go really well. He began to list the many activities he thought for sure she would engage in during the day.

*"Comment tu t'appelles?"* Jack asked for her name.

*"Myriam,"* she replied, drying her sniffles with her *mouchoir,* which she then placed back in her pocket.

MaryAnna stood silently as Jack talked calmly to the little girl. When she said her name, MaryAnna thought it was the most beautiful name she had ever heard.

Jack told Myriam that MaryAnna was nervous too because she couldn't speak French. Myriam expressed great interest in this tidbit, and her tears dried up almost completely. She found it extremely fascinating that someone would come to school and not even be able to speak! Immediately she set herself about the task of teaching MaryAnna to say *Bonjour*. Her efforts made MaryAnna laugh because this word, at least, she already knew.

While every fiber of Jack's body felt the need to stay close to MaryAnna, he made himself tell her good-bye and walk back down the path toward home. It was a chilly day, and the leaves rustled overhead in the gentle fall breeze. He felt a lump develop in his throat, and he begged God to bless MaryAnna's first day of school. He shuddered at the image of the way she looked when he left: clutching Myriam's hand, her face slightly pale and very serious. *Surely she will be okay,* he thought. *It won't take her any time to learn French, and her teacher speaks some English.* He had faith that God would take care of her.

---

Jack's thoughts returned from that September day to the present one in November as he parallel parked next to the sidewalk in front of the *salle*. MaryAnna had adjusted to school and was beginning to speak French very well. He knew that eventually she would speak much better than he ever could. *She might not even have an American accent!* he thought. Already her presence in the school was bringing them new ways to connect with the people in the community. And now he was returning to leading their team and its fledgling church here in Nantes. Ben had been doing all of the visiting by himself as well as most of the preaching and teaching during his two-week absence. Jack was eager to resume his duties. *Coffee. I must get the coffee pot started,* he thought.

The door squeaked open loudly as he pulled his key out of the keyhole. He walked into the entrance and opened the door into the main office, where the interns served as secretaries most mornings. He was surprised to see Alice sitting at the desk, typing away furiously on the typewriter. She was so intent on her work that she had not heard him come in. *She must be typing ninety words per minute! Not too bad for an amateur,* he mused. He had hoped for some peace and quiet, so he was slightly annoyed that she was already there. Usually the interns didn't arrive until mid-morning. There was just no need to push them to come in early, since very little work had to be done first thing in the day. *So what could she possibly be working on so arduously at this hour?*

"Alice?" he said loudly, attempting to be heard over the click-clacking of the typewriter keys. No response.

"Alice!" he said louder this time. More finger-pecking, as fast as her delicate hands could go.

"Alice!" he finally yelled.

The young intern jumped up out of her chair instantly and screamed. When she turned and saw Jack, she burst into tears and covered her mouth with her hands.

"I'm so sorry," Jack stammered. "I didn't mean to scare you. Are you okay?" In an effort not to be inappropriate, he decided not to hug her but simply stood his ground and waited for her to regain composure.

"I didn't expect to see you here so early," he continued after a brief pause. "I'm really sorry I scared you. I called your name twice before you heard me. The typewriter was too loud, I guess. Are you okay?" he asked again.

She sniffed and wiped her tears. "Oh, it's okay, Jack. I'm fine. I thought I would get a head start on the monthly report."

He was confused. The team usually sent a report to their supporting churches in the United States at the beginning of each month. They wouldn't be mailing it until the following week. It was something they often worked on together—he, Ben, and both interns—the Friday before mail-out day. Certainly not on a Monday.

*What could possibly be behind her sudden impulse to be excessively prompt and punctual?*

Unable to conceive of any logical reason for her strange behavior, he concluded in that brief instant that perhaps Alice was stressed because of Kathy's imminent return to the U.S. Kathy had suffered from a series of health issues since her arrival in Nantes and had decided to cut her internship short. She planned to leave at the end of the month. Alice, on the other hand, planned to continue to live in Nantes as a member of the mission team. Jack had worried privately about whether or not Alice had what it took to remain in a foreign country as a single woman, living alone in a downtown apartment building. *Perhaps the impending change is getting to her.*

"Alice, there is no rush on the report. We can work on it together in a few days when everyone is in the office like we usually do."

"I know. I'm sorry. I am upset because of something that happened back home. I woke up early this morning thinking about it and couldn't sleep. So I thought that I might as well come on in to work."

"Do you want to talk about what happened?" Jack ventured.

Jack waited as she composed herself to speak, wondering what he was about to hear and why it was affecting her so intensely today.

"I never told any of you here, but there was a guy back home. We dated pretty seriously for a while. His name was Jeffrey. We broke up before my decision to move to France, but I guess I always secretly hoped he would feel called to come here too, that we would fall in love all over again, get married, and have a family together in France. In my mind I knew it would never happen, but my heart couldn't stop hoping. Well, I just found out he is engaged to one of my best friends from home."

"Alice, I am really sorry. I know this news must be difficult for you. Tell you what. Why don't you plan to come over to our house tomorrow night for dinner. We can have a game night together, and if you want to talk about this some more with Marcie, we can do that too." Then remembering his home life, he added, "And, um, I hope you are okay with holding a baby for a while, if needed!"

"That sounds great, Jack. Thank you!" Alice smiled and wiped her nose and eyes with her handkerchief.

He was relieved to see her smile, albeit weakly.

"Now, in my opinion, there's only one thing to do when you haven't had a good night's sleep."

"What's that?" she asked.

"Coffee!"

They laughed and headed toward the kitchen to prepare some of the coffee he had stocked up on at *Euromarché* several weeks before baby Thomas's arrival. Cup in hand, he left her with the brewing pot and went upstairs, where the offices were located. *Managing these young interns who may or may not mature into missionaries is part of the job*, he thought.

Jack entered his office and looked through the small, square window at the street below. He noticed his parking job was particularly good that day. The rain had subsided a little, and the drenched tree branches were pelting water loudly on the roof of the *salle*. The dripping was pleasant. It was much more relaxing, he thought, than a crying baby, dirty diapers, and an active two-year-old, which was what Marcie would face today while MaryAnna was in school and he was at the office.

He watched Ben's car turn the corner on the north side of the street and roll toward the building. In contrast to Ben, it was Jack's habit to park catty-cornered from the main entrance of their meeting place, in front of the *boulangerie* (bakery). He would often stop in for some croissants or *pains-au-chocolat* (croissant stuffed with chocolate). He enjoyed the taste but also appreciated a chance to interact regularly with the workers and customers. *Perhaps God would move them to spiritual curiosity one day as a result of his visits,* he told himself.

Ben headed directly to Jack's office. "Hey brother! Welcome back," he bellowed. The two exchanged a few short family updates and immediately moved on to church business. Much had happened while Jack was away. The most recent Sunday morning visitors Jack knew about, but he'd missed the Tuesday night Bible study the previous week, and apparently a new face was there too. It was exciting news. Another visitation call would need to be scheduled.

Jack informed Ben that he and Marcie were planning to host the Tuesday night Bible study the following week. He knew Marcie had still not completely recovered from the baby's birth, but Ben and Amy had been hosting the Bible study for six weeks straight, and Jack did not want them to feel overly burdened. Ben agreed with the plan.

# CHAPTER 12

The first day without Jack's help at home was coming along nicely for Marcie. She had arranged to walk her neighbor's grandson Damien to school every morning along with MaryAnna (and Isaac and baby Thomas in the baby carriage). In exchange, the neighbor, Mr. Panard, would bring MaryAnna home when he brought Damien home. *Soleil Levant* Elementary School hours were nine to noon, followed by a two-hour lunch break, and then two to five. So Marcie walked the children to school twice every day: first at 9 and then at 2. Mr. Panard delivered them home twice a day: first at 12:15 p.m. and then at 5:15 p.m.

Today Marcie was feeling very proud of herself for having made such a creative arrangement. It was five o'clock, and Thomas was taking a nap. *How perfect*, she thought. *This will give me just enough time to get dinner started before MaryAnna and Jack come home.* She went into the kitchen and took a skillet out of the cabinet to brown some meat. Isaac was in the family room, playing with his cars. *I was made for these moments*, she thought to herself. Having three children was a dream come true. How strange, it seemed to her, that motherhood could feel like a millstone around her neck one day and a gentle spring breeze the next!

The meat sizzled as it turned from pink to brown. She spun her lazy susan and selected her spices with habitual ease: oregano, parsley, and basil. She cranked her can opener around the tomato containers and opened a jar of spaghetti sauce. As she did so, her mind wandered to MaryAnna. She hoped her day had gone well. She prayed for her for the hundredth time. The first few days of school had been a little rough for everyone, including Marcie, who had cried the first three days herself. She remembered with a smile how poor MaryAnna had returned home at noon on the first day, thinking herself completely finished with school. "I did it!" she said. "Bless her heart," Marcie whispered out loud. But MaryAnna proved herself to be tough and brave. She was adjusting well, and though she still sought out her teacher and stood by her for the first ten minutes of every morning as the children waited to enter the school building, she was beginning to make friends and speak French quite well after only three months. *It is so much easier for children to learn a foreign language than adults*, Marcie thought as she stirred the bubbling sauce.

She decided she would allow the older children a treat after dinner tonight. She'd opened the snack cabinet just an hour earlier to be sure she had one more package of gummy bears stowed away. At that moment Thomas had spit up and pooped simultaneously, so she'd had to run to change his outfit, leaving the snack cabinet door ajar. As she went back to the snack cabinet now, she discovered that the package of gummy bears was nowhere to be found. *Did I lay it on one of the counters?* She checked but found nothing. It was such a small thing, she realized, but Isaac especially loved them so much.

*Isaac!* She refrained from hollering out his name and stood stock-still. Putting her wooden spoon down quietly beside the boiling water for the noodles, she walked stealthily out of the kitchen and into the hallway. To her right were the stairs, where Isaac sat. She listened as the two-and-a-half-year-old voice murmured over and over again, "I'm gonna tell my momma I ate those gummy bears."

She and Jack had been struggling with Isaac's telling lies. Her heart leaped with pride at the thought of her son overcoming his weakness. Even though her evening surprise was ruined, at least Isaac was learning to tell the truth. Before she could go to him and ask him what happened, the doorbell rang. *Oh, why can't that man learn to knock? Doesn't he realize we have a baby here?*

Marcie rushed to answer the door, hugged MaryAnna, and thanked Mr. Panard. As she helped her remove her *cartable* (backpack), she couldn't decide whether to ask MaryAnna about her day or finish the business of the gummy bears with Isaac. But she didn't have time.

Every now and then, MaryAnna struggled with impulse control. At the moment, she was experiencing a mixture of relief to be home from school as well as curiosity about cuss words in French, some of which she had heard that day. After hugging her mother, she suddenly turned around, grabbed the front door knob, opened the door, and yelled, *"Eh Damien!"* Much to Marcie's horror, MaryAnna then hollered, in a freakish, dare-devil of a moment with perfect French pronunciation, *"Merde!"* ("shit").

For about three full seconds, nobody moved. Not even Isaac, who didn't have a clue what that word meant. Nothing Marcie had read in any of her parenting books could have prepared her for this scene. Did her four-year-old missionary daughter just yell a vulgarity, loud and clear, for everyone to hear?

Her paralysis was broken by Mr. Panard's laughter. He was belly laughing. He waved and mumbled something French about what a cute little *coquine* (rascal) she was. *"A demain!"* ("See you tomorrow!") he cried out and walked away.

MaryAnna, after her moment of brazen speech, knew immediately from her mother's reaction that she had made a grave mistake. Why, she wondered, did so many of her school comrades say that word if it was so wrong? She could see that the answer to that question mattered little in light of her mother's wrath.

Marcie was livid. She knew that in France, the word was tossed about much more flippantly than in the U.S. Children used it to wish each other good luck even though it was considered a "dirty word" in the States. She continued to be baffled by the odd French culture differences. She had certainly never encouraged such nonsense as shouting cuss words to friends for fun, nor would she ever! She marched into the kitchen and grabbed the wooden spoon she had planned to stir the noodles with. Anger and embarrassment flooded her. The blissful motherhood moment she'd experienced earlier had evaporated into feelings of mortification. Without any hesitation, she commanded MaryAnna to bend over right then and there, and she delivered a good wallop on her bottom. In her anger, she was tempted to turn and do the same to Isaac but realized she had not yet given him a chance to fully confess his wrongdoing. Was this the right time to ask him what he had been doing on the stairs? Would he be too terrified to tell the truth?

MaryAnna began to cry. Baby Thomas started to wail too. Isaac resumed his earlier blubbering of the "I'm gonna tell my momma I ate those gummy bears" refrain. And at that moment, in walked Jack.

After a brief exchange of looks, including a mix of desperation, exasperation, and bewilderment, Marcie ran upstairs to get Thomas. Jack sat down on the bottom step, taking turns asking MaryAnna and Isaac what was wrong. MaryAnna whimpered softly while he tried to coax Isaac into confession. Eventually he got the whole naked truth from Isaac, who admitted to eating the entire package of gummy bears, not just a few. As for MaryAnna, he told her firmly that she was never to use that word again and held her as she cried.

---

After the children were in bed, Marcie wiped spaghetti sauce off of the kitchen table while Jack swept the floor.

"Marcie, have you talked to Alice lately?"

"No, not since she brought some fresh zucchini over the other day."

"She is going through a hard time. Some old boyfriend just got engaged to one of her close friends. I told her she could come over tomorrow night for dinner."

"Still making appointments without consulting me first, huh?"

He scolded himself for not having considered her when he invited Alice. "I'm sorry, Marcie. I guess I got carried away again thinking about ministering to Alice. I should have called."

"It's okay, Jack. I would love to have Alice over. And I'll try to talk to her when she comes over and make sure she's okay."

"Marcie, God must have sent me an angel when He sent you to me."

"An angel who talks too much, who loses her temper with her children, and who is still carrying some baby weight?"

He measured his words carefully as he answered her questions in sequential order. "Maybe to the first, sometimes to the second, and Marcie, you had that baby only three weeks ago! You look like a million bucks. Really. I'm so thankful to be on this adventure with you."

---

The following day passed quickly for Marcie with more diaper changing, laundry washing, and meal planning for Alice's arrival that night. Jack came home early to help with the preparations.

Alice was at the front door at 6 p.m. sharp and was greeted with squeals of happiness from MaryAnna and Isaac, who loved having guests over to the house. Alice was very fond of children, and was happy to play and entertain while Marcie finished setting the table.

During their simple dinner of American-style beef stroganoff, Alice seemed quiet. Jack offered to put the kids in bed so that Marcie and Alice could talk. The ladies sat on the couch together with warm chamomile tea in hand.

"Alice, Jack told me about what happened. I'm so sorry."

"I didn't really think that it would work out between my boyfriend and me, but I couldn't ever seem to stop hoping. It's for the best really. Now I can finally move on."

"I suppose you're right. That is a very brave thing to say. It took me a long time to get over my first serious boyfriend in college. I thought I would never recover."

"Really? You? Marcie Jones?"

Marcie laughed.

"You think too highly of me, Alice. You are a precious girl. I believe that you will find the right guy at the right time."

Alice suddenly became quiet again. Then she ventured: "Do you think I should go back to the U.S.? Do you think I have what it takes to stay here and be a single missionary? I feel like I will be terribly lonely without Kathy . . ."

Marcie put her tea cup down on the side table and put her arm around Alice.

"Alice, that is something to pray about, for sure. You are welcome at our house anytime you feel lonely. But only God can tell you what to do about your future."

Alice's eyes became moist. "You're right. I sure wish someone could just tell me plainly."

Marcie looked at Alice and spoke with confidence. "Alice, God will show you. You just have to ask, then wait and listen."

When Jack came back down the stairs, the two women were sharing funny hairdresser stories. After a few minutes more of conversation with Jack, Marcie and Jack began stifling yawns. Alice realized that it was time for her to go home.

"Oh Jack," she said, "one more thing."

"What is it?"

"Well, François has invited me to come to his house a couple of times a month and discuss biblical things with him and Pauline. He feels like it would be really good for Pauline to be able to ask questions to another woman, and he knows that Marcie and Amy stay busy with children and other church work. Do you feel okay about this arrangement?"

"Well, yeah, sure. Keep me posted on how things go. Let me know if you start to feel uncomfortable in any way. I think as long as the three of you are together and you are on top of the questions, it should be fine."

"Thanks, Jack. I think this is just what I need to get my mind off myself." With that, Alice bade them goodnight and drove away.

Marcie and Jack headed right to bed. Thankfully Thomas chose to sleep all night. But early the next morning, when Jack's alarm went off, his thoughts floated back to the night before. He felt a strange sense of foreboding about Alice's request to spend regular time at the home of the Forresters, but he wasn't quite sure why.

*Jack,* he chided himself, *at some point, you are going to have to loosen up and stop worrying so much. If you want to be bold and courageous, you must stop fretting about everything that seems a little different or new.*

He got dressed in the dim light of early morning and headed for the coffee pot in the kitchen. *Even so,* he continued to himself, *it is definitely something to pray about.*

# CHAPTER 13

During a morning meeting in late November, Ben asked Jack how he felt things were going with François. The two of them had continued to meet with him after his baptism, and he seemed to be growing in his faith. Jack said he felt François was by far their strongest member and the one with the most potential to be a leader. He had a gift with the people there and could relate to them in ways that the Americans could not—because he was just so French, in spite of being British. Ben said he had the same thoughts, and he also felt that they should approach François and ask him if he might prayerfully consider joining them on the team.

Jack was hesitant. Although he had entertained ideas of François becoming a leader, he hadn't really pictured him as a full member of the team, at least not yet. He had pictured him instead in a secondary position of sorts. Certainly he was open to the team widening, but François would need to go through formal training first. And even if he agreed to do so, Jack had to admit to himself that the notion of François joining the circle of the inner workings of the church made him uncomfortable. *What if François wanted to do things that went against what he and Ben believed was right?* He and Ben had found a certain rhythm, and he was not eager to disrupt it. *Two's company,* he thought. *And what about Pauline? Would she be an example to church members like Amy and Marcie were?*

"Ben, I'm not sure I am ready for that step, and I am not sure François and Pauline are either. Are you implying that we might ask François to quit his job and come on full-time? If so, how would he support himself?"

"No, Jack. I think he could be an active member of our team and continue as a volunteer, not paid. He could have more input. It would be good preparation for him to become a deacon or elder of the church, for instance. In order for our church to grow, it is necessary for our team to grow as well. We discussed the idea of building self-sustaining teams with local leadership in our church plants before we ever left St. Louis. Do you remember? What if God is ready to use this couple in more ways than He is right now? Even though François is British by birth, he is practically French. In my mind, he is a perfect person to have on the team. Think how he can relate to people on a level that we may never be able to! I say we

95

contact William Langford, head of the internship program at McAlister Road, and see about François attending an intensive training session there."

"Hang on, Ben." Jack envied Ben's boldness and initiative personality. But it seemed to Jack that he was sometimes too spontaneous. "I remember what you are talking about with self-sustaining teams. But what if we push François too soon? Or what if he begins to teach things that we don't agree with?"

"Jack, at some point we have to take some risks."

Listening to Ben's reasoning, Jack felt compelled to set aside his misgivings, at least in part. "Ben, you are right. But before we do anything, we need to take time to pray about it."

"Jack, of course we should certainly pray about it. But is something else bothering you? I know sometimes you tend to be negative about new opportunities."

"That is not true!" Jack snapped, surprised at his own annoyance. *Why is Ben arguing with me?* Ben's answer to his unspoken question came before he could ask it aloud.

"I just want to challenge you to yield your own will to God's. Sometimes God brings things out of left field, and we have to be ready and willing," Ben said.

Jack felt stung. He told Ben they could talk about it more later.

------

During his drive home that evening, Jack stewed over Ben's words. *How dare he patronize me with the challenge to remember previous conversations in St. Louis about teamwork and question whether I was open to God's will? And I'm most certainly not negative about new opportunities!*

As he pulled into the driveway at home, he muttered a forced prayer. "God, please help us to make the right decision about François. Help me to be open to Your will." As he did so, he thought of the passage he'd read that morning during his quiet time. It was Proverbs 27:17, "Iron sharpens iron, and one man sharpens another." *Perhaps Ben is right. I am by nature very analytical, and sometimes I might come across as being negative about new opportunities.*

He searched his spirit. He was jealous of Ben's boldness. Ben invited new people and often took initiatives within the team. *Why*

96

*can't I think of this stuff sometimes?* Jack wondered. The progression within team dynamics always seemed to follow a pattern that Ben initiated. Jack longed to be the one to lead in that way. He knew that Ben was a gifted leader in a different way than he was, and envy sometimes crept into his soul, masking him to what actually needed to be done. He asked God to free him of the negative emotion that he felt for his friend and teammate. He then asked himself if he would be willing to take this new risk if that was what God wanted him to do. He vowed to consider the idea in a more positive light.

---

A few weeks later, Jack came to agree with Ben about inviting François to join the team, initially in a limited role and then later with more responsibilities. Around Christmas of that year, the two of them talked with François. He was very honored and accepted the offer with gratitude. Soon afterward Jack arranged for him to go to St. Louis for a short, two-week training seminar.

When François returned from training and began his new duties, Jack and Ben were pleased to see that François offered a unique teaching style that the French identified with very well. He was willing to learn from Ben and Jack, and eager to accomplish any task set before him. He took some pressure off the two missionaries by taking regular turns teaching and preaching, and even visiting the sick.

François and Pauline were an important asset to the growing church. With their help, the church grew spiritually, numerically, and even financially. Although growth was still slower than Jack wished, he continued to adjust his expectations from what they were when he set out for the mission field fresh from St. Louis. He could clearly see God working for the good of everyone.

During the next two years, the mission team nurtured the church and sought the Lord together. Three more interns from the U.S. came to join them short term and added more energy to the group. As another Christmas approached, the Joneses decided to take a much needed three-week trip to the U.S. for the holidays, leaving the Wilsons, Forresters, and four energetic interns to handle the leadership together.

# CHAPTER 14

On December 18, 1982, Jack, Marcie, and the kids were en route, flying TWA from Paris to St. Louis, and MaryAnna was sick. She suffered from every kind of travel sickness: plane, train, and car. This time Isaac was sick as well. Marcie and Jack both held vomit bags at the ready. Marcie also had to keep Thomas settled. Thankfully he was a very laid-back child and easily entertained. He played quietly in his seat with the wing pin the stewardess had given him when they boarded as Marcie and Jack helped each other clean up from MaryAnna's latest upchuck.

The nine-hour flight from Paris had gone well enough, but this one from New York to St. Louis was a killer. The children were exhausted, and there was still another flight to go from St. Louis to Little Rock. How Jack wished that they could have had a direct flight into Little Rock from Paris. Traveling was harder and harder with each new child. He checked his watch. *One more flight.* He prayed silently as he gathered items they'd pulled out of their bags during the flight, all the while trying to comfort MaryAnna. Her misery had shifted from her stomach to her ears, which were hurting so badly she began to cry.

"Marcie, do you want to give her some gum?" Jack asked.

"No, it will make her sick."

"Good point. How's Isaac?" He saw that Isaac lay on Marcie's lap.

"Asleep. Just in time for the landing," she said with weary sarcasm.

The pilot's voice came over the loudspeaker, announcing information about connecting flights, departure gates, and terminals: their next flight from St. Louis to Little Rock was on time. This news was disappointing to Jack. He had hoped for a slight delay. Their current flight had itself been delayed an entire hour, putting them in a time crunch to make their connection to their final flight to Little Rock. He was familiar enough with the St. Louis airport to know they would have to move very rapidly indeed. And speed of movement seemed impossible with a couple of sick children, a toddler, and four carry-ons.

He had been struggling lately with feeling a certain distance between himself and the Lord. It was unsettling to him. *Have I been following my agenda too much?* he wondered. At the same time, he thought how changed he was from the young man who once thought he could evangelize all of Europe and have twelve children. He was content for now to reach Nantes and possibly another city in France within the next few years. He also had plans to schedule a doctor's appointment to close a nice, gentle door on bearing any more offspring. *Twelve children? What was I thinking?* The three children they had were worth everything it cost them, but the price was high. Life was a constant balancing act, and he now had a more realistic view of what he could handle.

With pride, Jack reminded himself that the *Église du Christ* in Nantes had seen twelve baptisms since Thomas was born two years ago. *Victory! So why do I feel emptiness now? Am I not faithfully continuing on with what the Lord wanted me to do? Or am I supposed to be somewhere else by this time, moving more rapidly on God's plan for my life? Why must I be plagued with such thoughts even when circumstances are good?* He had to admit, he had been in Nantes long enough to slip into a rut of activities from time to time. He knew he needed fresh motivation, new ideas. But what?

The leadership team had door-knocked several times with different campaign groups. The church was growing, but in his mind it was painfully slow. And half of the members seemed like "fruit buckets." Marcie had shown her claws once when one of them, a single, middle-aged female who seemed to always need to talk to him, had come to their home one day asking for *Jacques.* She told Marcie she was going through a really hard time and was desperate to talk to him. Marcie took it upon herself to tell the woman *Jacques* was not available, and that if she wanted to talk to someone, it would have to be her. Marcie had been around long enough to know where certain women were headed. Jack grinned at the memory.

He shifted his position, with MaryAnna lying down and resting her head on his leg. *Perhaps the Lord will enlighten me with fresh motivation on this trip.* In the meantime, he told himself, he would just be thankful for the change of scenery that a trip home would bring.

The aircraft hummed loudly as the wheels unfolded from its underbelly. MaryAnna cried through it all, ignoring the loud thud from the wheels touching down onto the tarmac. She retched again into the airsick back. Jack stroked her hair. As they approached the terminal, she finally settled down, although she said she couldn't hear anyone. "When you talk to me, it sounds like you're in a tunnel, Daddy," she complained.

His thoughts began to wander again but stopped abruptly. *How are we going to make the connecting flight?* He had no idea. He and Marcie were exhausted, and MaryAnna said she still felt sick. He was truly at a loss. Perhaps they would just have to take a flight the next morning and check into a hotel tonight. No. He resolved at least to try to make the connecting flight. Perhaps it would be delayed at the last minute. It was worth a shot.

He decided to carry Isaac and let Marcie hold Thomas. He gave MaryAnna a pep talk and helped her put on her backpack. She would have to be brave. He would coax her into hurrying. Together as a family, they stepped off the plane and onto the loading bridge.

As they approached the terminal, Jack saw familiar faces from the past—what seemed to him like a dozen of them. They were friends from Jack's internship days. *What are they doing here? How strange. They must have heard we were flying in through St. Louis. Boy, it sure is good to see them!* How he wished he could stay and have a cup of coffee with each one of them!

Jack's longtime friend and old roommate, Don, gripped his arm and said, "Listen, we heard you were passing through this airport briefly, and we wanted to spend time with you during your layover. We didn't realize there would be so little time between your flights. By the time we got here, we realized y'all would need help. So here we are! We're going to help you make your next flight. I'll take this one. She looks a little green."

Don grasped MaryAnna's hand and then hoisted her into his arms. As if in slow motion, Jack next felt Isaac's weight shift to the man next to Don, his old friend Rob. Another took Thomas out of Marcie's weary arms. There was no time to allow himself to bask in the bliss of the moment. He could hardly believe what he was seeing. If it hadn't been for the fact that he knew every face surrounding his family, he would have thought these were angels sent straight from heaven. Tears formed behind his eyes. The Lord was reaching down through a soft whisper of friends, reminding Jack that He *was* with him, taking care of every detail. Although there was very little time to walk to the next gate, to Jack, time stood still. He felt God's

100

presence again through these friends. It was as if they had just lowered him down through a roof to see Jesus!

The men carrying his children began running through the airport. Their wives ran alongside Marcie, who was too incredulous to cry. One of them had taken Marcie's carry-on for her. The rest ran behind. The running caravan was humorous, but to Jack and Marcie, it was beautiful.

With two minutes to spare, they boarded the connecting flight to Little Rock. As Jack stowed their carry-ons, he thought about the words from Hebrews12:1, "Therefore, since we are surrounded by so great  a cloud of witnesses, let us also lay aside every weight, and sin which clings so closely, and let us run with perseverance the race that is set before us."

# PART IV

# Sowing Seeds

# CHAPTER 15

"The land of the free and the home of the brave" was a delight to Jack and Marcie's eyes. They had forgotten how much they missed Doritos, Cheerios, red licorice, Cracker Jack boxes, and root beer floats in a frosted mug. Christmas dinner did not disappoint either, with the traditional turkey, gravy, mashed potatoes, green beans, homemade rolls, dressing, pumpkin pie, pecan pie, and chocolate Eagle Brand pie. For the kids, there were colorfully decorated cutout sugar cookies and mouth-watering chocolate drop cookies along with mounds of candy.

In France, Father Christmas would fill little French clogs with treats and leave children a reasonable one or two Christmas gifts. Here in America, Santa Claus stuffed stockings to the brim, and boys and girls woke up to toys spilling out from piles stacked under Christmas trees. Even the neighborhoods and city streets screamed out holiday cheer with elaborate decor. Gifts of clothes, toys, and as many accessories as they could fit in their suitcases were lavished upon the Joneses.

The differences between France and the U.S. were suddenly astonishing. Americans donned brightly colored clothes and big hairstyles with huge bangs—while the French remained entrenched in muted colors with fashionable edges of leggings and leather pants. By far the most obvious dissimilarity between the two countries was the religious inclination. America's government hinted at strong Christian values, which the French regarded with cynicism.

Jack and Marcie appreciated their American roots for many reasons, but they also had come to enjoy many aspects of French life, such as less emphasis on materialism and excess in exchange for more simple pleasures, a more reasonably paced life, and French gastronomy, envied worldwide.

---

When the family returned to the airport in January, they felt reenergized and recharged. The return trip was less eventful than the flight in. As was typical for the time of year, it was rainy and cold when they landed in Nantes. The weather didn't matter much to them though. They were so exhausted by the time they reached their house on *Rue des Magnoliers* that all they wanted to see was the inside of their bed covers.

Thanks to Marcie's foresight, the sheets on the beds were clean. It was heavenly to slip inside them. Even the hum in their ears leftover from being inside an aircraft, miles above the ground for over eight hours, didn't bother them as they drifted into a deep sleep. In a way, the trip to America felt like a dream. They would awaken the next morning to the reality of their lives in France once again.

During the first few days after their return, Jack and Marcie continued to compare cultural differences. The French were not known for modesty, but why did they have to display topless women on life-sized billboards to advertise yogurt? Also, it seemed that on certain days, everyone insisted on being rude, no matter how nice Jack and Marcie were to them. On market day, though, Marcie collected her fresh goods for the week and was able to push past "a multitude of sins." When it came to food, there was really no comparing to America. First was the bread: *Baguette, Pain de Campagne, Ficelle, Batard, Croissants, Brioche.* Then the cheese: *Brie, Cantal, Camambert, President, la Vache qui rit, Babibel, Boursin.* The pastries, other baked goods, pâtés, sausages, and succulent dishes and recipes such as *boeuf bourgignon, galettes, crêpes,* and *tarte aux pommes* were delectable. But best of all was the bread.

Jack and Ben had always been happy to contribute regularly to the income of the baker next to the *salle.* Thankfully they were both still young and had high metabolisms, so the daily *croissants* didn't seem to bulge their thin middles. One cold January morning as they went over to the bakery to indulge in their morning pastries over coffee, Ben listened with interest to Jack's report of the time in the States.

"So, are you ready to move back home yet?" Ben chided.

"You know, Nantes is beginning to feel more like home than America in a way," Jack replied, thinking sheepishly of the extravagances they had enjoyed recently. "Why can't we learn from the French when it comes to keeping holidays simple? It's ironic that we are the Christians, and yet our home country insists on over-commercialization."

Ben pondered his response and smiled. He had missed hearing Jack's analysis of life.

"And now to the *Église du Christ.* Catch me up, brother!" Jack begged.

"Well, François is doing great. I can't wait for you to hear him speak now. He's a natural. I think he is almost ready to take over for us!"

Jack knew his friend spoke in jest, yet he fought back jealousy at the thought of someone else changing his leadership role.

"François has such good instincts when it comes to church work," Ben continued with confidence.

"What about the interns?" Jack asked next.

"They are doing great. Alice spent Christmas with the Forresters. She seems very close to them now. They have taken her in as if she is part of their family. Several times a week, it seems, she comes into the office and tells me all about the fun evening she had at the Forresters' house the night before."

Jack thought about this new development and felt happy for Alice. He remembered her asking him what he thought about her studying the Bible with the Forresters. At the time he had felt slightly uncomfortable with the idea. He stifled the thought.

"Everything sounds perfect," he managed to say. "Maybe I should go away more often!" His words teased with more truth underneath the sarcasm than he cared to admit.

"I guess there is one thing that worries me," Ben said.

"Oh?" Jack said, listening with renewed interest.

"It's Pauline. She doesn't seem as eager to help with the children anymore. She seems a lot more subdued, even sad at times. It makes me wonder if she is hiding something from us."

"Do you think it's just that she misses her family? Holidays are often hard when there are family issues. Do you remember how her family disowned her when she became a Protestant?"

"That must be it," Ben exclaimed with some relief. "I can't believe I didn't think of that. Jack, I've missed you, brother."

Jack's confidence was restored, and he felt light again. It felt good to reassure his friend, to be useful. And yet he wasn't sure that he himself was fully buying the reason he offered for Pauline's malcontent. *Was something deeper going on? And what about Alice's sudden happiness at the same time? But then she had always been a bit flighty,* he thought to himself. He couldn't quite figure out what was making him feel uncomfortable about this new development. A cheerful voice interrupted his thoughts.

"Hi, Jack! Welcome home!"

"Hi, Alice! I hear you are doing well!" Jack replied, startled to see her at the café.

"I am!" she replied exuberantly.

Jack motioned for her to join them at the table. He couldn't help but notice that she seemed different. Had she matured? He wondered if she had changed before the Christmas holiday and he simply had failed to notice. Regardless of when the metamorphosis had taken place, she seemed less silly. Ben had told him she was more focused on the work at hand, acting less like a tourist and more like an adult, always willing and able to lend a helping hand. Never in a million years would Jack have predicted that Alice, the goofy American girl who had practically proposed to a Frenchman by accident within a month of the interns' arrival, would outlast her quieter, more intellectual, and more soft spoken counterpart, Kathy, who was now back in the States.

Alice was pretty, and though Jack was not tempted by her looks as some men might have been, he recognized that she was an attractive young woman. She had white-blonde, shoulder length hair and bright blue eyes that were friendly and inviting. She wore glasses, but only when she read, drove, and worked in the office. They sat on her soft, small nose, enhancing rather than distracting from her appearance. Her skin was fair, her teeth perfectly white, and she had a smile that lit up a room. She could be on a Swedish advertising poster for milk or cheese, Jack had thought when he first met her. She always looked healthy, happy, and Nordic. She smiled almost all of the time, even when carrying on regular conversations. Everyone seemed attracted to her butterfly personality. Although she had seemed too outgoing and naive to Jack when she first arrived years earlier, he had come to appreciate the way she cheered up the bitter folks and comforted the sad ones in the congregation.

Despite her love for all things French, Alice remained steeped in her American blue jeans and brightly colored T-shirts—except on Sunday mornings, of course, when she usually donned a straight skirt and one of her many form-fitting sweaters. She was always generous with her make-up, and not uncommonly had a small swab of lipstick on her teeth first thing in the morning. Today she looked particularly bright-eyed, even glowing. Jack wondered again about her newfound happiness and the amount of time she was spending with the Forresters. *It was wonderful, of course, wasn't it?*

"Oh! I almost forgot to tell you!" Ben said, bringing Jack back from his musings about Alice. "This letter came while you were in the U.S. It's been sitting on my desk for a week now. It looks interesting."

Jack looked at the letter. The envelope was covered in pictures of mountain countryside. No wonder Ben thought Jack would be interested. He quickly opened it. It was an advertisement for anyone interested in becoming a certified summer camp director in France. Licensing would be granted at the end of a weeklong training seminar in Marseilles.

Growing up, Jack had spent most of his summers at Camp Deer Run in Texas, where he was both a camper and then a counselor. He smiled at the memories of campfires, scary stories, the traditional Sadie Hawkins' night, camping in the woods, softball games, devotionals, grilling hot dogs and marshmallows, and sweating like a pig from the summer heat. Those were the days!

*This could work!* he thought immediately. Perhaps if he were certified and the team trained, they might reach the younger generation. It was certainly worth a try. He stuffed the letter in his pocket, and the three of them headed to the office.

---

It wasn't until Jack was home in the evening that he returned to his thoughts about Alice and Pauline. Perhaps it was just his tendency to be overly negative or worried, but he couldn't shake the feeling that something was amiss. As he spoke with Marcie about the matter, she reassured him that Alice, their intern who had been with them the longest, had always acted very responsibly, and that if Pauline was upset, Alice would be the perfect one to help comfort her. Marcie encouraged him to try not to make up new things to worry about.

As he was reading a bedtime story to the children, his mind wandered.

"Daddy, you skipped a page," chided MaryAnna.

He corrected his mistake, robotically reading *Oh, the Places You'll Go*, by Dr. Seuss to the end for the hundredth time.

By the time the book was over, he had managed to work himself back into worrying about work. *Could François be doing something that might subvert the work of the church? Is that what was worrying Ben about Pauline's behavior?* He tried to talk himself out of the dark intuition. He would try to talk to Ben about it more at just the right time. And most certainly, he would pray.

Days turned into weeks, but the right time never came. Jack ceased to feel the need to pursue the perceived problem anymore. When he shared with the team the idea about the camp, they received it with enthusiasm. He and Ben invited François to join them in the camp training venture. All were equally excited to see what God could do with this newfound opportunity.

# CHAPTER 16

Saint Patrick's Day arrived in the dregs of winter, dreary and cold. Ben, Jack, and François set out for the camp training. They boarded the TGV, *Train à Grande Vitesse,* bound for Clermont-Ferrand, in *Puy-de-Dome*, part of the region of Auvergne. When they arrived, they took a bus to the training facility. It was once a boarding school in a village called Vitrac in the Massif Central Mountains located in the middle of France. An old stone wall surrounded the camp's three main buildings. Vines crawled up the sides of the buildings. Deep in the countryside and hidden from civilization, the setting was breathtaking, and the three men immediately noticed the milder climate.

As they removed their luggage from the belly of the bus, they saw a group of four older men who were smoking pipes and playing a game of *pétanque* (similar to bocce ball) in a sandy pit nearby. They listened to their banter, *"Je la tire ou je la pointe, Joseph?"* ("Should I roll or toss the ball, Joseph?") and *"Ah, tire-la, tire-la donc!"* ("Well roll it, roll it then!") The sun would soon be setting, and somewhere a French mother was cooking *steak haché* (ground steak). They could smell it from a distance through her open window. A couple of children rode by on bicycles. The weight of city life began to evaporate. The three made their way to the main building to register.

*"Bonjour, messieurs! Je m'appelle Maxence Dubois."* After introducing himself, Maxence, the desk clerk, assisted them in filling out paperwork, instructed them on meal times and lectures, and then showed them to a rustic bunkhouse that looked to be about a hundred years old or more.

*"Alors, voilà, je vous laisse"* ("I will leave you, then"), Maxence announced and then cheerfully turned to leave. The three men stared at each other in disbelief. This was obviously a coed space. François didn't seem shocked or bothered, but Jack and Ben felt uncomfortable.

"Wait, Maxence!" Jack called out in French.

*"Oui?"* Maxence waited politely.

"Sir, if you please, where are we supposed to stay?" His face must have registered shock and also what Maxence interpreted as disdain.

Maxence's reply hinted mild annoyance. He answered with his best English. "I know that our bunk houses are rudimentary, but they are satisfactory and sufficient as far as cabins go. If you require more, then you should find another place to train for camp counselors. Please show a little more appreciation for an opportunity to be in a natural environment."

Jack was growing uncomfortable. Surely Maxence could understand his mistake in neglecting to ask them if they preferred coed or all men's rooms. His reply was conciliatory. "No, not at all, sir. We are very grateful. But we would like to stay in the men's only cabin, if you please."

"This is all we have, sir," Maxence answered curtly and turned to go.

Ben and Jack looked at François, uncertain as to what to do next.

"It's all right," said François. "You'll get used to it. You just try not to look."

The three of them turned to see a woman undressing right in front of them. When she saw the men turn their eyes away, she teased them. "What's wrong? Have you never seen this before?"

She wrapped a towel around herself, stepped outside, and crossed the path to the bathhouse. When she opened the door to the showers, they could see a row of shower heads out in the open with no separation in between.

Though Jack and Ben had preached and taught countless lessons about standing up for what was right and not giving into peer pressure, it now felt extremely awkward and uncomfortable to do so. They returned to the front desk to plead their case. After Maxence called them lunatics and immature for asking again for different accommodations and said there were none, the three of them decided to do their best to handle matters on their own.

Each night they waited until all of the others went to bed and then took turns standing guard in front of the door to the bathhouse so that they could shower out of female eyesight. It made for short nights, as many participants were out very late. By the third night, exhaustion was wearing them thin. As they sat outside the bunkhouse, they prayed, asking God to help them stand firm.

"Praise the Lord," the answer came, soft as a whisper to each of them.

112

Jack began to sing, and the other two joined in, quietly at first. Some fellow campers walked by, acting as if they didn't even see them. Others made derogatory remarks. Jack, Ben, and François felt strange and out of place, like beggars on the street who made passersby uncomfortable. No one, however, told them to be quiet. Emboldened, they sang a little louder. They sang together until the bathhouse was free.

---

Jack was thankful for the opportunity to get up close and personal with the French people. They participated in many physical activities, forcing everyone to move past the barriers of personal space, including tug-of-war, relays with eggs, water balloon fights, and soccer games. With the rich resources Jack had to draw from out of his Camp Deer Run experience, he quickly became a popular source of new ideas for the rest of the group. The French found his innovative American ideas most intriguing.

"Look," Jack instructed one evening after supper, "take your stick and shave the end to make a sharp point like this." He illustrated with his pocketknife. "Then, use the sharp point to pierce your marshmallow and slide it onto the stick. When it is well roasted, put it between two cookie crackers and add a piece of chocolate." They loved s'mores. Jack always lost his audience, however, when he talked about devotions around the campfire. They had no aspirations of encouraging campers to pray, hear words from the Bible, or sing religious songs. If their campers were to sing anything, they told Jack, it would be nonsensical tunes such as *"Un kilometer a pied, ça use, ça use"* ("One kilometer on foot wears out your shoes for good").

On the very last night, Jack, Ben, and François had a small gathering of six fellow trainees around them to listen to their nightly serenade. The three men were touched that God had cracked a door open in this rural setting. They resisted the temptation to burst the door wide open and share the gospel openly for fear that the small seed being planted might be trampled before it had a chance to sprout, choosing instead to wait for God's timing and His prompting on the hearts of these few. They sang the same songs they had sung the previous nights, and then ever so gently, as if lifting a baby bird back to the nest, they asked if anyone would like to know more about why the three of them believed in Jesus. At this point, half of the gathering left, but three stayed. Well into the night, the three men from Nantes shared their faith. They answered questions about who Jesus was and what He did. Two of the sets of eyes stayed mostly dim the whole time. One face, however, was changed. He asked if he might stay in communication with them, giving them his contact information.

After their last covert shower, Jack, Ben, and François lay wide awake in their bunks, pondering over the thrill of sharing Jesus in this place. François was on the bunk directly above Jack, and Ben was in another bunk against the opposite wall. Ben fell asleep first. Jack was beginning to feel the heaviness of sleep settle over him in the darkness when he felt the bunk above him shake.

*François must have rolled over,* Jack thought. He began imagining returning to his own bed in his comfortable house on *Rue des Magnoliers* and felt a shake again. *Maybe François has to go the bathroom,* he thought. He felt more awake now, so he listened intently. He heard stifled sobs.

"François?" Jack whispered, staring up at the wooden planks on the underside of his friend's bed.

François was quiet.

Being a father of three, one of whom was still an infant, Jack was used to wake-up calls. He stood up and looked at this British Frenchman who had become his friend. "Want to talk about it?" he asked.

The two of them slipped quietly into the darkness outside.

"I can't believe it," François began, his voice shaking as he fought for control of his emotions. "How could God let this happen?"

Jack was at a complete loss. He had been riding the high of being used by God to reach a lost soul. *What could François possibly be talking about?*

"That man tonight . . . " François's voice trailed off.

"I know. Isn't it tremendous? God opened a door here!" Jack thought that perhaps François was simply full of joyous emotion.

"No. I mean, yes, it is, but I don't deserve it. Not any of it. I don't deserve to be a part of this or anything else we are doing."

Jack was flabbergasted. "François, you can't be serious. Why are you saying this? You have every bit as much a right as I do to be here. God has made you an integral part of the church."

"No, Jack. I don't deserve it." He paused and then added, "I need to confess something to you."

Jack's stomach lurched and turned hot. He remembered his fears about Pauline and François and was overcome with dread as he listened to his friend's confession.

"When I was eighteen, I attended *Sorbonne* University in Paris. Some of the people I hung around with there were not good for me."

Jack's mind reeled as fuzzy thoughts filled his brain of trying to imagine François as a teenager.

"One of them was a guy who lived in my apartment building, across the hall from my room. He only lived there for a year."

His voice became weak again. He swallowed hard.

"He had a secret stack of magazines hidden under his bed. One night as I was visiting with him, he showed one to me. It was a new one, he said. He had just received it that day. He tossed the magazine over to me and said, 'Take a look at that, big boy. You'll never be the same.'

"He was right. I can't explain what happened to me. Something inside felt strangely guilty yet incredibly fulfilled. My relationship with God was dormant at best, so it didn't take me long to become addicted to that feeling. I even got angry with my friend one day because he was supposed to have a new issue and hadn't gone to check his mailbox.

"After a while, I became disgusting to myself. My shame became too much for me to bear, and I became depressed. And then somewhere in the middle of it all, during my last year at the *Sorbonne*, Pauline walked into my life. She was lovely and pure. She was my savior, I thought. I was inspired to kick the addiction. I never told her about it. We became engaged and were married soon after we graduated. But after about a month of being married, the old desire came back. At first I just tried to tell myself things would get better the more Pauline and I got to know each other and got used to each other, if you know what I mean."

Jack's mouth was dry. He managed a nod.

115

"By the time we had been married two months, I gave in to my old temptation. We had moved to Nantes, where I started working for *Leclerc*. I found a store on my way home one night. It was an adult store. . . ."

François stopped as he choked back a sob.

"I'm telling you, I don't deserve any of this. When you baptized me in the *Erdre* River two and a half years ago, I told myself I would never go back. I knew it was wrong, and I was sure God would help me stay pure. And believe it or not, I lasted two years without indulging in the old temptations. But last year, I fell again. And it's worse than ever. Every night, after Pauline goes to bed, I go downstairs and watch movies. So many of them . . ."

François halted again, overcome with grief and self-loathing.

"Jack, I need to step away from leadership. I'm sorry to let you down. I will talk to Pauline. I need help. I have sinned in an enormous way. I have not been faithful to my wife. I'm nothing! I would rather wallow in my own filth than continue to live the life of a hypocrite. Do you hear what some of these people have said to us this week? That it's refreshing to be around us because we're not hypocrites like the rest of the religious people they know?"

In the long, awkward pause that followed, Jack said nothing. He was aghast. *Conversations like this one were supposed to happen with new converts,* he thought, *not with coworkers or teammates.* His heart was filled with shock and anger mingled with sadness. Although he was relieved that his friend's confession did not involve a secret plan to take over the church work, he had no words of comfort to offer. He wanted desperately to find the solution to this ugly problem. "Lord," he prayed silently, "help!"

"It's okay, Jack. You don't have to say anything. I need to step down from serving as a leader. My mind is made up. I don't want to continue to allow 'sin to be in the camp' like Achan did in Joshua 7. You preached on that story just this past Sunday: about how Achan took some of the devoted things and because of that many Israelites suffered and died at the hands of their enemies. I do not wish to hold the team back because of my sin. It's time to purge it from the church so that I do not stunt any growth in *Église du Christ de Nantes*. I am going to confess to Pauline and then also to the church, if you feel it is necessary."

Jack's silence continued as he wrestled with the news, first with the impact on Pauline. *Surely Pauline suspected. How could she not?* Like Ben, he had noticed Pauline was quieter and more subdued. *No wonder. Perhaps she thought if she said anything, she would put her husband's integrity in danger.* It was not her nature to confront anyone, let alone expose her husband. *She must feel terribly betrayed. And even if she forgives him, François has a long road ahead of him, whether he stays on as an active member of the team or not.*

Jack's next thoughts were about the team. *What will Ben and I do without him if he leaves?* He remembered how resistant he had been to François joining the team a couple of years ago. Now he didn't want to go on without him.

"François, wait," Jack stammered at last. "You have been a Christian long enough to realize that God forgives. We just have to find a way for you to be more accountable."

François resisted Jack's offer at first, but as they talked further, he agreed to not make any rash decisions in the middle of their last night of camp training when they were so exhausted. He agreed to meet with both Ben and Jack again on their first day back at the office together. The three of them would pray together and seek the Lord's guidance.

They returned to their bunks, both needing to get some sleep. They had a long day of travel home the next day. After some tossing and turning, Jack's combination of anxious thoughts and a tired body gave way to slumber.

---

At dawn, when the bright and beautiful sun rose above the bunkhouses of Vitrac, François asked Jack to speak to Ben for him about his confession from the night before and then left for the bathhouse. Like Jack, Ben was shocked and overwhelmed with the potential impacts of the news. When François returned, he managed to put his arm around him and said they would certainly talk more about it when they returned.

François didn't eat or drink anything until they arrived at the train station in Nantes. Jack thought it strange to see him so subdued. He almost always wore a smile on his handsome face. His somber countenance cast a shadow on the other two. As for himself, he had a headache, bags under his eyes, and felt slightly nauseous. His *Grand Crème* and his *pain-au-chocolat* purchased on the homebound train had not been enough of an anesthetic.

He thought about the demeanor of so many of the *Nantais,* who seemed to have little hope. Shadows hovered over them. He felt as if a sinister force was swallowing them up in its dark vortex, as if they were being made to submit to a giant machine that had its clamps firmly around the nation of France, robbing its inhabitants of the life that the Father intended for each of them. Without knowing it, many had accepted the hypnosis of the evil one. They operated throughout their days as if God didn't exist. *If only they knew how much He longed to remove the shield from their eyes!*

Jack shook himself out of his depressive trance. *No! I will not succumb to this temptation. I will not give in to these negative thoughts.* He began to quote Hebrews 12:1 to himself: "Since we are surrounded by so great a cloud of witnesses, let us also lay aside every weight, and sin which clings so closely, and let us run with perseverance the race that is set before us."

---

The train delivered them back to Nantes, and Jack drove the trio the rest of the way home in his *Deux Cheveaux,* dropping Ben off first. When he pulled up to the Forrester home, on an impulse and out of desperation, he finished the Scripture passage he'd been ruminating on for hours in his mind, saying the words of Hebrews 12:2 aloud. "Looking to Jesus the pioneer and perfecter of our faith, who for the joy that was set before him endured the cross, despising the shame, and is seated at the right hand of the throne of God."

François looked at Jack, startled by the sound of his voice and the words of Scripture. His eyes began to glisten. The two sat in the car as the motor idled.

"François, if there is any need for me to forgive you for what you have done, then you have my forgiveness. And if I can forgive you, how much more will God do the same? You have a repentant heart, and I know you have a long journey ahead of you. But we can get through this together. A race has been marked out for us. Let's run it together. Don't give up now."

Jack saw a hint of the old François as his friend's mouth began to curve into a faint smile. Outside, through the bright sunshine, it began to rain. The world around them turned a strangely glowing, golden color. They both felt God's presence seeping through the clouds and into their hearts.

François assured Jack he would talk to Pauline. He agreed they wouldn't make any drastic decisions yet about him stepping down from leadership. Jack prayed as he watched François opened the door to his home.

When he pulled up to his own house on *Rue des Magnoliers*, Marcie was holding Thomas on her hip, standing in the open doorway. MaryAnna was in front of Marcie, waving her arms wildly around in a greeting to her daddy, who in her little girl heart was the best in the whole wide world. Isaac was poking his head around from behind Marcie, pushing Marcie slightly out of the way so he could join his big sister. And sensing the excitement, Thomas began to bounce himself up and down, grabbing at Marcie's shoulders and burying his head in her neck.

---

Pauline did not struggle with François's confession as much as Marcie or Amy might have if it had been one of their husbands. Although her Christian walk had taught her differently, she was used to the French mentality about sex: that it was very natural, married or not, and however one chose to indulge. Plus, she claimed that she already knew about his sin struggle. Over time, however, she became bitter toward François, holding his sin as leverage over him to manipulate him into doing whatever she wanted him to do. The Wilsons and the Joneses put in many hours counseling and helping to restore the marriage relationship. Other truths began to surface, one of which was the fact that the Forresters had been hoping for a child for almost ten years. The failure to conceive had placed more strain on an already delicate marriage.

Pauline didn't seem as interested in Alice meeting with them quite as much as before, so the intern made herself scarce. Marcie met with Alice to make sure she was okay, but she seemed aloof and uninterested. She had so much enjoyed her friendship with the Forresters, but now Pauline showed no interest at all in their Bible studies together. Marcie knew that this would hurt Alice's friendship with them. But Alice always changed the subject when Marcie broached it and so it was dropped.

# CHAPTER 17

Ben and Jack encouraged François to continue in his vigilance every day and to stay on the team. They watched as God used his weakness to make him stronger. He submitted to their authority, thankful for forgiveness and a second chance in ministry. In time and with God's help, he was able to encourage a few other men in the congregation who confessed they had similar struggles.

It was a long time before Pauline resumed her natural charisma and energy, but she eventually forgave her husband fully.

Spring and summer smoothed over the wrinkles leftover from the crisis. As fall approached and the leaves lost their green luster, preparing for the annual wintry death, Jack and Ben received a letter from their beloved McAlister Road Church in St. Louis.

September 22, 1983


Dear field workers and faithful seed sowers,

I applaud you for the efforts we have been reading about in your report letters. I eagerly await an opportunity to come and see for myself the wonderful work that you have begun in the city of Nantes, to which you were called by God.

I have put much thought and prayer into what I am about to reveal, and I am very unsure of what steps God would have us take to remedy the problem. Please read and be in prayer for wisdom.

Two years ago, two families much like the both of you came together and pledged to commit themselves to the work of the Lord. They felt called to Rennes, about 70 miles north of Nantes. Their launch date was set for the beginning of June of this year. Unfortunately the wife of one of the families lost both parents in a plane crash a few weeks ago. For understandable reasons, this couple pulled out of their commitment to the Rennes mission.

The other family, the Morses, fasted and prayed for their partners and grieved with them. When their partners decided that they would no longer proceed with the plan to move with their teammates, the Morses laid their plans before God and asked for an answer as to what they should do. They felt strongly that God led them to proceed with moving to Rennes, and that He would provide a partnering family to work alongside them. They did not know the time frame, but they trusted God for His provision.

I am encouraged and amazed by their faith. I am also concerned. My belief is that no missionary should set out alone. But God may have other plans. I trust Him.

I have tried to figure out what can be done to assist this family. At the very least, I want to make you aware of this development. Perhaps one of you could plan to visit them upon their arrival? I know this news is somewhat disturbing, and I hope it doesn't come at an inopportune time. I have no specific instructions for you, your team, or your church. I see you as equals and trust that God will impress upon you any action that might need to be taken. Please know that you are in my prayers, as are the Morses. I pray that God will reveal to each of you the steps that you must take and give you the strength to take them.

Your brother in the faith always,

William Langford
Honored to serve as Elder,
McAlister Road Church of Christ


Jack and Ben shared the news from the letter with their wives that evening. It brought an uneasy feeling that change was upon them. Who would God provide for the Morse family? Was it time for one or both of their families to go and help another family in a new location? Was the Lord orchestrating this change?

Jack and Marcie slept fitfully that night. Marcie woke up nauseous. She was nauseous all day and suspected a virus. Jack woke up in a cold sweat. He stayed home to help with the children and kept mulling the letter over and over in his mind. He had dreamed that he and Marcie were packing boxes and getting ready to move to Rennes to help the Morses, but it just didn't feel right. He knew that if God was calling him, he would feel peace, not dread.

The next day when he went to work, he found Ben already at the office. They didn't speak of the letter until lunchtime. Ben spoke first.

"I did not sleep well last night," he said. "The truth is, Amy and I are wondering if the Lord is calling us to help this family. For the past several months, Amy has been telling me she feels like the Lord is preparing us to move. I have resisted her because I did not have that same feeling. I have loved being in Nantes and I know the Lord led us here. Amy, however, has continued to meditate and pray on those passages from Genesis, the ones about God calling the patriarchs away to a land that He would show them, and we feel that they are for us now as well."

Jack was not prepared for this news. "But Ben," he managed to say, "surely you can see God called us here together. What about the day that you and Amy prayed for a sign for me when I sought out Nantes and Strasbourg? We have barely begun to establish the work here in this city."

"I believe beyond a doubt we were supposed to come with you to Nantes. But perhaps it is now time for a different destination. Haven't you wondered if one of us would feel called to help this family?"

Jack remembered with a shudder his dream from the night before. He did not share it with Ben.

"Who knows?" Ben continued. "Perhaps if we go, God will move us again from there so that we will remain 'nomads in the land.' Each of us must go where God leads us, regardless of how difficult it seems. I am not saying that we are going to move as soon as the Morses arrive, but I am going to ask God to make it very clear to us whether or not we should go and if so, when. "

Jack's heart sank. He could hardly believe what he was hearing, and yet somewhere deep inside of him, he knew that one of them would feel called.

"What if I am the one supposed to go?" he said. "What if you are supposed to stay here? Perhaps I am the one not being open enough to the Lord's voice."

"Jack," Ben said with confidence in his voice, "I know God will show one or both of us what He would have us do: go or stay, move or be still. I believe that He is faithful and that He will make it clear. Don't you? Who knows? Maybe when you pull into your driveway tonight, you will be given a sign as to whether you should go or stay."

Jack knew Ben was right. And yet he felt tremendous sadness. When he returned home from work that day, he looked at his door, hoping he might see a sign on it that said "GO" or "STAY"

122

in large letters. Instead he walked into a house in disarray. Marcie was nowhere to be seen. MaryAnna was playing a game with Isaac, and Thomas was making his racing cars drop off the kitchen table over and over again. The kitchen looked as if it had not been touched since breakfast. Dishes were piled on both sides of the sink, and there was open food everywhere.

*Oh no,* Jack thought, *Marcie must have felt sick again today. I wonder if she has the flu.* He greeted the children, thankful that they were settled, and walked upstairs with a quick pace. Marcie was lying on their bed with a trashcan at her bedside. She rolled over to see him walk in the room, revealing a face full of tears.

"Oh, Marcie, I'm so sorry," Jack said and sat down beside her to caress her hair. "What can I do?"

Marcie pulled a tissue out from under her pillow and wiped her nose. She obviously had been crying for a long time.

"Do you want me to take you to the doctor?"

"I have already been. Amy came over to watch the children this afternoon."

"Oh, good. Did he give you any medicine?"

"No." Marcie broke out into a fresh sob. "I have a condition that you cannot medicate, and it will not go away for nine months."

Jack listened carefully.

"Marcie, my love, are you . . . ?" His mind reeled as he recalled his intentions of following through with the doctor's appointment that would have eliminated the possiblity. He had put it off one too many times.

"Pregnant," she said, "again!" She buried her face into her pillow.

He smiled in spite of himself. "Marcie, this is wonderful news!"

"Oh, Jack, how can you say that? We decided to stop having children. Why did the Lord choose to bless us with another one? I know this sounds terrible, but I don't think I can do it again. I don't think I am strong enough. I don't feel like I have the patience or the stamina. Look at the three that we have. Thomas is just now potty trained and coming out of the baby stage. I'm not ready to go all the way back and do it again, Jack. I'm just not ready!"

She blew her nose into her tissue.

"Marcie, I have been unsure about many things today, but one thing I am sure of. You are strong enough. God will give you the strength. And I am going to do everything within my power to help you. You are not going to go through any of this feeling alone. For starters, I want you to stay here the rest of the evening and let me take complete control of the kids, the kitchen, dinner, homework, baths, bedtime, and everything else. I'll bring you some tea. Oh Marcie, don't be sad that God chose to give us one more. He or she will be precious. You will see."

She buried her face in her husband's shoulder. "Jack, I don't deserve you. Why are you so good to me? I know I will love this child. I already do. I am just so overwhelmed."

Jack walked downstairs to the three musketeers now playing hide-and-seek. Once he had dinner brewing, Ben's words rang in his head as clear as a bell: "Maybe when you pull into your driveway tonight, you will be given a sign as to whether or not you should go or stay?" *Moving at this time would be extremely hard on Marcie. God had both closed a door and opened a tiny new window.*

---

Soon after the Morses arrived in the city of Rennes, the Wilsons and the Joneses made the trip there to greet them. Within a few weeks, the Wilsons' growing conviction that they were to move to Rennes turned into a decision. The Nantes team, including the Forresters and Alice, met to pray together for both the old and new teams. On the St. Louis front, William Langford recruited several single interns who were eager to enter into the mission field. He informed the Wilsons and the Joneses that three were coming to the Nantes team and three were coming to the Rennes team. Alice was thrilled.

On the morning of the Wilson's departure, Jack helped Ben load the last few boxes into the moving truck. Despite the sunny morning, sadness threatened to choke him. The time had come to say good-bye.

"Jack," Ben said, "don't underestimate the gifts God has given you. Amy and I are praying for you and Marcie, that the Lord will provide more support for you and the team here. I believe He will do that. Hey, I'm just following your dream to help evangelize all of France, you know? And then all of Europe and then the world, remember? You still have that heart. And Rennes is not far. We can have combined church retreats once a year or maybe even twice! Not to mention the coffee shops between here and Rennes. I expect you to figure out which one is the best and meet me there as often as possible."

A hush came over the two men.

"Ben," Jack finally said, "thank you for supporting me the way you have. The years spent with you have been some of the best of my life."

Jack had tried not to think about what his mission would look like after Ben left because, frankly, he didn't know. As he watched Ben lock the door to his house for the last time and step toward his car loaded to the brim, he felt a lump in his throat. He tried to hold back his emotion until he was safely back inside his own house.

Ben turned to wave. Jack waved back at the man who had accompanied him overseas, who always had so much hope in his eyes, so much faith; the man who had been at Jack's side through thick and thin; the man who had laughed him through countless trials and helped him "chalk it up" when they had to deal with draining church members, or "basket cases," as they called them; the man who had challenged him when he needed to be challenged. Ben had the boldness that he himself lacked. He had helped to make his burdens light. And now he was leaving. Jack waved back.

"Love you, brother," Jack said.

"Love you too, brother," Ben replied.

# PART V

# Ugly and Beautiful

# CHAPTER 18

MaryAnna loved the month of December. It was her birthday month, her brother's birthday month, and Christmas all wrapped into one. In ten days, she would be ten years old. Four and a half years had gone by since her daddy's French training camp to become a director. This year she had been old enough to attend the *Camp Colonie Harmony* in Languedoc-Roussillon, a region in the Massif Central Mountains, and for the first time, she had stayed in a cabin with girls her age instead of in her mother's cabin. She had such fond memories of her time there with other Christian girls, and often she thought of those times during these cold winter months.

Only six more schools days separated her from a holiday season full of celebrations at home. Today everyone in her class was making an ornament. The teacher helped each child cut out foam circles. MaryAnna's were pink and purple. Each circle was then pierced in the center and placed on a string with needle and thread.

MaryAnna followed the teacher's next instructions carefully. She made five strings of threaded foam circles. Her teacher then helped her tie them together: one string became the main string, two other strings were tied close to the top of the main string and two others strands were tied at the bottom of the main string. Altogether it was intended to look like the body, arms, and legs of a miniature decorative person. The teacher then helped her attach a ping-pong ball for a head. Finally, a foam, cone-shaped hat was placed on top.

As she skipped along the familiar path from *Soleil Levant* school, MaryAnna bounced her ornament man up and down. Because she was in the fifth grade this year, called "CM2" in France, Marcie allowed her to walk the short, five-block walk by herself. She could hardly wait to show the ornament to her mom and dad when she got home.

The Joneses had moved into a new neighborhood two years prior, mostly to accommodate the newest member of the Jones family, Caroline Ruth. Baby Caroline had made her entrance into the world despite Jack and Marcie's decision not to have any more children. Now none of the family could fathom the world without her adorable, thumb-sucking, blue-eyed, blond-headed self. She came out of the womb with an agenda. She watched her siblings carefully, idolizing each of them. She desired to emulate each of them in her own way. MaryAnna immediately took on the role of a second mother to her and thought of her as her own living doll much of the time.

MaryAnna was eager to show her daddy her pink and purple man craft. She had been telling him about it every day, updating him on her daily progress and insisting they place it on the Christmas tree when she brought it home.

"Of course we will," he'd said.

MaryAnna broke out into a run as she rounded the last curve to *Impasse Blandine*, the street on which the family lived. The tips of her shoes dug into the gravel at short intervals as she bounded toward the front door, then shoved her left shoulder into it while turning the door handle.

"Dad!" she shouted at the top of her lungs.

She was met instead by an angry mom, whispering sternly, "SHHHHHH! You'll wake up Caroline!"

"Oh, sorry, Mom!" MaryAnna replied weakly. "Is Dad home yet?"

"No, darling. You know he is not usually home until suppertime."

"Oh, well he came home early yesterday!"

"Yesterday was an exception. What are you so excited about, MaryAnna? How was your day at school?"

MaryAnna eagerly held up her finished craft. But just as Marcie began to praise her accomplishment, Caroline cried out from her bedroom, "Mommy!" and began to whimper.

"Sorry, Mom."

---

Jack was minutes from home, driving the family's Volkswagen utility van. The *Deux Chevaux* had finally died and was replaced with a larger family car. He missed that old yellow car. It held many memories of the beginning of their lives as missionaries. Parallel parking, one of his specialties, was a challenge now in such a bulky auto, but he could still do it.

He was pensive during the drive home. It felt like a very long time since he, Ben, and François had attended the seminar for camp directors—four and a half years ago. And now the Rennes and

130

Nantes missionary teams were in the process of planning their third annual *Camp Colonie Harmonie* in the South of France.

Though he had lost Ben to Rennes, God had been faithful to provide him with three new interns who had decided to stay long term.

"Jack," he said out loud to himself, "you have every reason in the world to be happy. You have a beautiful wife who loves you and four wonderful, healthy children. You are pursuing your dream as a missionary in France. You have François to work alongside you as coleader plus four energetic interns. What else could you want?"

He had missed Ben terribly during the months following the family's departure four years ago. At the time he had felt very doubtful about what would happen to the team. But William Langford had sent Bruce, Angela, and Suzanne from McAlister Road Church to help with the transition. Bruce was a gifted teacher and speaker, Angela had a heart for women's ministry, and Suzanne enjoyed working with the children. Although no one could replace Ben Wilson, the combination of François's maturing and the giftedness of these new team members softened the blow of losing such an integral part of the church. Alice, who had been with the team for six years, was no longer viewed as an intern. She had given her life to be a mission worker just like the Joneses, Wilsons, and Forresters.

François had proven himself to be trustworthy. Though he admitted to Jack that the old demons of lust came to torment him every now and then, he seemed to be holding them at bay. He had filled in the hole left in Ben's wake as if he himself was a missionary veteran.

Although François was remaining accountable to Jack for his daily activities, something had been bothering Jack about him recently. Of the past six preaching opportunities Jack had offered him, he had turned down four of them. The first two were sickness related, but the reason for the last two remained a mystery to Jack. He knew he should extend grace to his coleader. Besides, he had other resources—the three new interns plus Alice. The two occasions when François mysteriously refused to speak turned out to be good opportunities to allow Bruce, the male intern, to speak. *I must ask François about this matter soon,* he told himself.

In spite of the overall good climate of the church and the smoothness of the season of life within which he currently found himself, Jack occasionally struggled to overcome melancholy emotions. For no apparent reason, the weight of the world would make its way to his shoulders, and he struggled to throw it off. Although the children were growing more excited by the day about the arrival of the Christmas season, it just felt like chaos to him. He was not exactly looking forward to all of the noise that usually accompanied the multiple, joyous occasions of the month of December.

So it was with slightly slumping shoulders that he darkened the door to his house at *31 Impasse Blandine* at 6 that evening. As he entered, MaryAnna practically jumped onto his briefcase. She dropped her craft and almost caused him to step on it in her excitement to show him her masterpiece. He did not produce the reaction MaryAnna had anticipated. Instead, he gave her a weak hug and a request to show it to him later. Caroline was next, with her lisped greeting, "Daddy'th home!" Jack tossed her up into the air and caught her just in time to feel one boy grab his right leg and another bigger one grab his left. He suppressed his desire to escape into a newspaper and leaned into his children. After a few minutes of rough and tumble, he went into the kitchen to kiss Marcie. MaryAnna trailed close behind. He slumped into a chair at the table and asked Marcie about her day.

Marcie knew something was bothering him. "What is it?" she asked. "You have that look again, like you are carrying a pack full of bricks."

"Oh, I don't know, Marcie. I wish I'd snap out of it."

MaryAnna came in and sat down at the kitchen table with her daddy, placing her craft on the table in front of him. Jack's eyes caught hers. She couldn't hide her nervous smile. Without being able to control herself, she began to laugh. Jack broke out in laughter too. *She has been waiting to show me this all day*, he thought.

"Okay, MaryAnna," he said, "let me see your ornament."

As MaryAnna showed him her craft, he could see how excited she was. He remembered helping her pierce the hole in the ping-pong ball so that she could bring it to school the next day. She had been so frustrated because she could not figure out how to poke a hole by herself. To him, it was simple, of course. He'd talked to

132

her about the importance of being happy and not always fretting and worrying.

He had almost forgotten what it was like to be that excited about something. *That's it! I need the same lesson I taught her last week about being happy. Starting today, I'm just going to decide to be happy.*

Her voice droned on about how her teacher had helped her tie the five pieces of string together. As she did, Jack felt his spirit filling up with hope. He listened to her with new interest and resolve. *It is as simple as the smile on MaryAnna's face,* he thought.

She finished her story about the craft and then went into the next room to hang it on the Christmas tree. Jack then listened attentively as Marcie told him about a conversation with Catherine Freslon, mother of Aurélien, the neighbor who was in Isaac's class. She was interested in coming to one of the church's Tuesday evening Bible studies. It was all very exciting to Marcie.

He pondered the agony and ecstasy of life: how things could look so bleak one moment and bright the next. He chided himself for forgetting that it was Tuesday and that he would be leading the weekly Tuesday night Bible study at their home that evening. He had not prepared a lesson for the occasion, but he was invigorated by Marcie having invited their neighbor. He could feel excitement rise within him at the prospect of meeting another lost soul.

The family sat down to a dinner of *Tranches de Dinde*— turkey slices stir-fried with tomatoes, green peppers, and onions served over rice. Jack led them in a prayer for their meal. "Dear Heavenly Father, thank you for always providing for us. Thank you for giving us new reasons to rejoice everyday. Thank you for comforting us and for bringing us joy when our hearts are sad. May Your name be praised. Amen."

---

After dinner, MaryAnna helped Marcie clear and wash the dishes. The boys were sent off to help Jack move the folding chairs stored in the garage to the family room and rearrange the furniture in the usual Bible study fashion. Soon what was a cozy living space became a hodgepodge of seats that included kitchen chairs, a sofa, folding chairs, and the piano bench.

The doorbell rang at 7 p.m., announcing the arrival of the first guest. Jeanine, who had been a member of the *Église Du Christ* of Nantes the longest, entered first. She always selected the most comfortable seat. An older retired couple who had been coming for about a year followed her. The Rondeau family showed up next with their three elementary aged children. François and Pauline then entered, followed by Alice and the other interns: Bruce, Angela, and Suzanne. Finally Catherine, Marcie's invited guest, arrived. Everyone greeted her warmly and made her feel at home.

Jack began with a prayer, Bibles were opened, and the study began. Within a few minutes, Jack and Marcie became uncomfortable, realizing that Luc Rondeau was intoxicated. His words were slurred and his comments were not appropriate. Jack was trying to determine which scenario would be more awkward: to ask Luc to leave in front of everyone or to allow him to continue in his current state? Also, they were starting a new series tonight on the book of Matthew, which began with the genealogy of Jesus in Matthew chapter one. And who had volunteered to read but the Rondeau's oldest teenage daughter, who was dyslexic! How awkward it was for everyone to wait patiently until the verses were read. Jack felt powerless to cut off the youth. And to top it all off, Jack became aware of gentle snoring noises. Jeanine had dozed off in her comfortable chair. *Of all things!*

Without asking for volunteers again, Jack requested that François read the next passage. He then posed questions about the life of Jesus and encouraged everyone to listen with an open mind for any new perspectives the Lord might want to reveal to them tonight. Robert, the older retired man, began telling about how he first heard about Jesus as a young boy while attending Catholic school. But he got off on a tangent about how his teacher liked to spank all of the girls. Pauline skillfully steered the conversation back on track and shared about how she had begun to see Jesus in new and different ways through teaching school. Her comment was a light in a sea of darkness at that point.

Jack and Marcie couldn't help but notice that Pauline seemed to be carrying a mysterious burden that night, a weight that was much too heavy for her thirty-seven-year-old shoulders. Dark shadows passed through their minds as they wondered about the climate of Pauline and François's marriage. Could the forces of evil have returned despite François's four years plus of accountability?

Discussion of Matthew continued as one of the children laughed loudly from the other room. It was Alice's turn to teach the young ones that night.

Even though Alice enjoyed getting to know Bruce, Suzanne, and Angela, the new interns, she did not bond with any of them.

After the Wilsons' move, François and Pauline had helped Alice find a more affordable apartment closer to where they lived. The Forresters had resumed their friendship with her and not infrequently had her over for dinner. Alice regarded them as her closest friends. She respected François's opinion on spiritual matters as much as Jack's, and she would sometimes ask to study with him after evening Bible studies.

When it was Alice's turn to take care of the children during the Bible study, she and the children always played silly games together in the children's rooms and had a grand time laughing and horsing around. It was all well and good, as long as it was reasonably contained. Tonight, however, it seemed a little more out of control than usual—probably because the Christmas holidays were imminent. Jack and Marcie wondered what their new guest, Catherine, must be thinking. Of all nights, she had come on the most uncomfortable, disorganized evening of Bible study yet.

The hour of study time passed by, albeit slowly. And the fellowship time felt endless. After everyone left, Jack and Marcie prayed that the night's events wouldn't be a stumbling block to Catherine's faith and search for the Lord. Jack encouraged Marcie by telling her that he had decided to be happy no matter what, and that all things are possible with God.

# CHAPTER 19

Jack woke up the next day anticipating the beginning of his exegesis of Romans. He had received a new commentary in the mail two days prior. It was better than any Christmas present he might receive. He decided to head for the office earlier than usual.

As he drove, he felt a stirring in his spirit. He was growing in his faith. God had brought him inner strength and the ability to persevere under trials. Losing Ben had been very difficult, but God had carried him through the loss. He felt stronger for it. His relationship with the Lord was firm, and he gleaned much energy and encouragement from his prayer life. He always found time to pray and meditate, and he felt himself rising above many of the negative things that he sometimes allowed to creep into his spirit and discourage him.

When he arrived at the office, he was surprised to see François's and Alice's cars there already. Occasionally François would come into the office on his day off to help Jack or Alice with a task or to meet with a member, but why so early, he wondered. He had noticed that François was meeting with Alice more and more frequently. When he asked about the meetings, François said they were studying the Bible together. Now a strange sense of dread fell on Jack. He remembered his conversation yesterday with François when he told him he was planning to start studying his new commentary today.

"Are you going to study at the office or at the coffee shop?" François asked.

"The coffee shop. Don't you know me by now, François?"

Jack had then remembered he would have to go to the office first so he could get an old commentary he wanted to compare with the new one. He was about to correct the small mistake by telling François he would in fact be coming to the office in the morning for a few minutes but then thought it not necessary. After all, François did not need to concern himself with the goings and comings of Jack to the very detail.

Now, as he looked at the two cars, he became concerned about Francois's motivation for asking him where he would study. He also remembered that because Alice's apartment had recently flooded, she had asked for and gotten Jack's permission to stay at the church for two or three nights until the carpets were dry. Panic seized him. He had been so focused on keeping François accountable in his struggle with pornography that he had not given other matters related to his behaviors much thought—including the inordinate amount of time he and Alice had been spending together.

"Wait," he said out loud. "I decided yesterday I was going to be happy. Why am I making up something to worry about?"

*Pauline must be here, not François. Perhaps she and Alice are planning something special for the holidays.* The thought brought a flood of relief. Last year Alice and Pauline had come to the church and baked four or five batches of American sugar cookies. They were a hit with all of the French church members. *Pauline must be taking a day off from her job to bake with Alice like they did last year.*

He turned the front door knob, opened the door quietly, slipped in, and closed the door behind him. He was hoping, with growing desperation, that he would hear two female voices coming from the kitchen along with loud clanging and banging of pots, pans, bowls, and kitchen appliances. He didn't.

He approached the stairs with dread. Dark thoughts passed through his mind, and he couldn't stop them. He suppressed an urge to turn around and drive home.

Halfway up the stairs, he heard noises. When he reached the top, the sounds were more audible. They were coming from behind Ben's old office door. They were gentle, and they made the hairs on the back of his neck stand up. He felt such intense shock and anger that for a full minute he couldn't move. But the horror of what was happening and the desire for it to stop jolted his limbs into movement. *How could they sin against God like this! And at church!* He wanted to burst in and scream at them. His mind went blank with rage even as he sensed God was empowering him with self-control.

Knocking on the door gently, he called out, "François? Alice?"

One full minute of silence followed without sound or movement. Finally the sound of shuffling of feet came from behind the office door. Something fell to the ground, a shoe perhaps. And then, as much as all three of them would have liked to avoid what came next, the door opened. There stood François, disheveled and barely dressed. Behind him was Alice, sitting on the office chair, looking equally disheveled, her face in her hands, sobbing quietly.

Jack forced himself to look at them. The muscles in his face were quivering with a mixture of embarrassment, wrath, loathing, sadness, and a gigantic question mark. There were no words.

Jack broke the silence, saying simply, "Let's talk about this later. You two should go home now."

After the adulterous couple left, Jack went into his office and sat down at his desk, aging a decade it seemed. His mind reeled as pieces to a disgusting puzzle came together quickly in his head. The times François reported not having been to work on a certain day because of a mysterious illness but recovered miraculously within twenty-four hours. François volunteering to bail Alice out whenever she locked herself out of her apartment, which seemed to happen almost every other month. And all the hours François and Alice had been spending in "Bible study" together.

Not knowing what else to do, he chastised himself. *Why did I not see the red flags? If I had, I could have confronted the problem before it got to this point.* He thought about Pauline. *How difficult this news will be for her.* He recalled with chagrin that he and Marcie had sensed Pauline was not happy about something, but she never opened up to them that she suspected anything. *She must have had some inkling. Why didn't I try to talk with her about what was bothering her? As usual, I was too busy focusing on my work.*

Unreasonable thoughts crowded the space in his head that needed so desperately to make room for reasonable ones. *Now what?* He began to think of quitting. He thought earnestly about it. He wondered how long it would take to sell his house. He wondered if he could get his job back in St. Louis working for the photo finishing shop while he pursued another career. *Ministry was a huge mistake for me. Look at what I allowed to happen right under my nose. And God? What in the world am I supposed to think about Him and His plans?*

His mind turned dark as he pondered the answers to ugly questions. Could the church make it without him? Oh, how tiresome it had been for him to be so patient and perseverant for these eight years while he gently guided the *Église du Christ* of Nantes! He couldn't handle it anymore. Could he go home, declare failure, and start a new life?

Somewhere deep inside, he felt the need to pray and listen to God. But his stupor of anger and self-recrimination caused him to ignore the urge initially. Instead, he allowed fear and worry to grip him. He had four children to think about. And what about Marcie? He had no idea how she would take it all. Marcie was a strong, godly woman. She had not hesitated to follow her husband in pursuing his dream. Would she agree to quit as well?

*Wait a minute. This really was* my *dream, wasn't it? Yes, God has been in it, but am I the one who thought it up and just asked for His blessing?*

He thought again about the time God had called him and Marcie to Nantes. It had been so clear then that the plan was God's, not his. He remembered the sign that Marcie and Ben and Amy had prayed for. How the French acquaintance of his, Serge, had appeared out of nowhere and asked him to come to Nantes. Even in his present darkness of spirit, Jack knew the Lord had brought them to Nantes. He had chosen the right path. But in this time of shock and grief, the future suddenly felt very unclear.

"God," he prayed, "should I stay on this path? Or is it time for a change?"

He listened in the silence of his office for hours. Uncharacteristically he skipped lunch and just stared out the window. The wind had blown almost all of the leaves off the trees, but one bird chirped as if no amount of drama, large or small, could alter its routine of gathering food in preparation for the coldest months of the year. The outside world was oblivious to the problems of a late-thirties missionary from Missouri who felt he was losing his way. He was desperate to hear God's voice. He was desperate to find the answers. *Where do I go from here? What should I do? Can the small team here make it? Will the fledgling church survive something like this?*

Somewhere in the middle of the afternoon, he got into his car to drive home. As he turned onto *Impasse Blandine,* the gravel road sounded louder than normal under the tires, and it jolted him out of his trance. Now he would have to walk into his house and fake being okay until his children went to bed.

No, not today. He couldn't do it today. Not on the day he felt like everything he had worked for was failing. The weight he carried was too heavy. Today he would be selfish. Marcie would have to hold things together for a few more hours. He would just let her know he was home from work and then go to his bedroom or maybe for a walk.

He opened the front door and Marcie was there. Almost without controlling his words, he began. "Marcie, we need to talk."

# CHAPTER 20

The weeks that followed were the most painful Jack had ever experienced in ministry. After François confessed to Pauline about his affair with Alice, she understandably chose to leave him for a while. Marcie was very concerned about Pauline and tried to reach out to her as much as she could, but she remained aloof and distant. Her already small frame became emaciated as she lost pound after pound from disgust, depression, anger, resentment, and bitterness.

Alice had flown back to the U.S. without addressing the church. She had written some of the members that she was closest to, explaining that something personal had come up and that she was unsure of when she would return.

Next was the matter of telling the church. Marcie and Jack tried to remain calm and steady when church members asked about the Forresters, who suddenly were not there anymore. Two weeks went by before Jack confronted François, saying someone was going to have to tell the church members something. He told him he owed an explanation to the small *Église du Christ* he had helped grow.

François begged Jack to speak for him. "I have nothing left to give. My sin is still so fresh. It nauseates me. I just wish I could die, except that I would be leaving Pauline. I have no real hope of my marriage surviving, but I will do everything within my power to save it. Please, Jack, I need you to address the church for me. Please just tell them that I am going through a hard time with Pauline. I think it would be okay to lie a little, don't you?"

Jack lost it. "You coward! Was it not enough that you perverted our entire mission all this time and right under my nose? How dare you ask me to bail you out of this thing that you have done? I will not do it. You dug your hole, now you find your way out. I thought you were accountable to me. I trusted you. How long have you been lying? I will not facilitate any more of your lies."

François hung his head, unable to respond. Jack continued, emboldened with anger. "If you do not tell them, the church will find out eventually. These things tend to come out in ways we don't foresee. But not this time. Oh no. You are going to tell them. You are going to tell them this Sunday. In two days. Do you understand me? You are going to tell them!"

Jack awoke Sunday morning with an ache in his belly. Christmas had come and gone. He and Marcie had tried to make sure that the children felt no ripples from the huge wave that was rocking the *Église du Christ* in Nantes. Today was going to be a big day in the life of the church. François was finally going to confess.

Alice was long gone, back to the United States. Up to this point, none of the church members had been told the true reason for her departure. Some were beginning to get curious and asked Jack what was happening. Finally Jack told them that they would understand at church today, that there was a special announcement to be made.

The morning Alice left, Jack had to visit the doctor because of a sinus infection. He was relieved to have avoided interacting with her again. Talking with her the day after he discovered her in Ben's office with François had been bad enough. She had sobbed through the entire meeting. He was quite sure the meeting did neither of them any good at all except for the fact that he could say he tried to reach out and prevent their work relationship from being completely severed. He had done his duty, and at this particular time in his life, that was good enough.

On the way to church, Caroline was whiny and crying because she had to leave her brand new Christmas baby doll behind. Marcie tried in vain to calm her by handing her books to look at during the car ride. The rest of them had to sit and listen to her whimper and complain. Usually Marcie would have quoted a Scripture to her such as Philippians 2:14, "Do all things without grumbling or questioning," but today she was content to remain quiet and let the Holy Spirit convict Caroline.

"Mama, I dollie! I dollie!" Caroline repeated over and over again.

Marcie just ignored her and fought the tears behind her eyes. *Lord,* she prayed silently, *we need a miracle.* She was weary of trying to stay strong for her husband. It took every ounce of her strength on most days just to take care of the children, get the washing done, gather food for their meals, cook and prepare nourishment a few times each day, change diapers, straighten up the house, take time to make herself look attractive to her husband, and

142

nurture her relationship with God. By now she was used to the usual flow of her or Jack going through mild down seasons. But this time was different. It was a time of crisis and the uncertainty of their future was weighing her down.

The Joneses arrived at church and filed in the *salle* in orderly fashion. François arrived at the same time and walked solemnly through the door after them, alone. When it was time for François to address his fellow believers, a hush fell over the church. He spoke slowly and carefully but with a blank look in his eyes. All of his emotions had spilled out over the course of the past month: passion, conviction, desolation, devastation, depression, desperation. He had little left.

His confession began just as it had with Jack four years ago in front of the bunkhouse in Vitrac, during camp director training. He told about his addiction to pornography. He told about how he had continued to fall back into sin from time to time during the years he was a member of the church plant here in Nantes, despite his accountability with Jack. And then came the part about Alice. It was gut wrenching. The expressions on people's faces were ones of incredulity. Many looked toward Jack as if perhaps he would speak up and say something to make everything better again. Much to everyone's horror and dismay, the naked truth was as real as the cold frost that had slapped them in the face as they left home for their morning commute. He finished by saying he was stepping down from the leadership team and was praying about whether or not God would have him leave the church.

By the time his speech was complete and he stepped away from the front of the church, people were aghast. Shock covered their faces. Jack, however, felt an unexpected sense of relief, as though he were in the eye of a hurricane. In the midst of such a great sin against God, the church, the team, and his family, François was doing the right thing. His only option now was to cling to God. Life as he knew it would never be the same. François had said he knew that God was the only One who could bring any sort of healing from such a tremendous mistake. And he was right. Jack believed it too. Inwardly he begged God to make a way for his friend.

Jack spoke after François, fully anticipating the need to deal with the gamut of emotions of the church members. He talked about being human, which meant making mistakes. He read the story in

John 8 of the woman caught in adultery. Never before had he experienced this story the way he did that day: inside the passage.

What happened next Jack could not have predicted. One by one, the church members began to confess their sins. Some seemed small: sins of bitterness of heart or of shunning a friend. Others were flabbergasting: abusing a spouse, trying to kill someone, attempting suicide, having sex outside of marriage. It was unbelievable. What Satan had meant for harm, God used for good.

Jack wiped his eyes from emotion and prayed out loud after each confession. During the final prayer, his tears began to flow freely. How was God bringing such tremendous victory out of the ashes of defeat? Surely he would never doubt Him again. Every time in his life he had come to a place of hopelessness, God had given him more reason to hope. He felt closer to God than he had ever felt in his entire life. He remembered the time when he had sat by that pool at Harding, all those years ago. He had thought his life was taking a downward turn, and then, out of the ashes, God raised him up. Once again, he felt like he could do anything with the Lord by his side.

After dismissal, the church members surrounded François and begged him not to leave the church. They now understood the reason for Alice's abrupt departure, but they mourned the loss bitterly. Some expressed their worry about Pauline and said they longed for her return.

François was swayed by such an outpouring of love and concern. Although he felt the therapeutic forgiveness of his fellow believers, he knew he must suffer the full consequences of his actions. If he was to entertain any hope of saving his marriage, he would need to devote himself to winning back his distressed wife and help her find healing. He wanted desperately to help her. He loved her still, but he knew that love would have to be proved over and over again. He would do all that it took. If he tried everything and she still refused him, then at least he could say he gave his all. Hope. He could always hope. Hope was all that he had.

Many church members wanted to know how they could help. Of course, there was nothing that François really wanted any of them to do except pray at the moment. This they pledged to do with all of their hearts.

On Monday Jack went home at lunchtime and decided to take the rest of the day off. He wanted to spend some time with Marcie and be there when the children arrived home from school. It was a much-needed respite from this new, unfamiliar path he found himself walking.

With Ben and Amy in Rennes, Alice and Pauline gone, and François's unpredictable future, Jack felt alone in the mission he had started with so much vigor almost a decade ago. He needed the balance of Marcie and the kids to counteract the loneliness he felt in the work of the ministry. Yes, Bruce, Angela, and Suzanne were still there, but his relationship with them was not as strong as it had been with the other ones. And it seemed like every time he built a close friendship, it was taken away from him. These interns were struggling with the news more than the church members. Perhaps it was because of the differences in culture, or because they were young and impressionable and had not been exposed to much of the world yet. Perhaps it was because their support back home (family and other close friends) were too far away for them to seek comfort. Besides, how could they reveal what was happening inside the church to their support network? The news would not reflect well on the church in Nantes they had committed to help. Jack knew that he and Marcie would need to try their best to be a family to them and listen to them as they struggled through this ugly reality of what life can be like in ministry.

That night, as he was tucking MaryAnna and Isaac into bed, he read to them from *Prince Caspian*, the second in a series of seven Christian fiction books by C.S. Lewis. He began at the point in the book where Lucy, Edmund, Peter, and Susan had all arrived in Narnia, a magical land, and they were trying to find their way to the "stone table" to help a good prince save Narnia from evil enemies. Lucy awoke in the night and encountered Aslan the lion (the Christ-like character). He urged her to come in the direction he was going and instructed her to go wake the others and tell them to come too. Lucy did not succeed in waking the others right away, so she reported back to Aslan.

Jack read Aslan's response, which was to tell Lucy she must follow him alone. Lucy was dismayed by Aslan's order. She did not want to leave the others behind. Even though she was reluctant to obey Aslan, however, she followed his instruction. The others eventually followed as well, but not until after Lucy stepped out on her own.

*This is what God is calling me to do*, Jack thought. *God is calling me to carry on alone.* The thought made him feel more alone than ever before. But he knew God still wanted him to carry on. Just like in the story of Gideon, when God kept on trimming Gideon's army to a smaller and smaller number, Jack felt as if God was trimming down the Nantes mission team.

"Am I not enough for you?" came the still, small voice.

*Yes, Lord, you are enough,* Jack answered silently.

---

The next day, Jack got up early and drove outside the city limits of Nantes to some old castle ruins. In and around the ruins were many mossy paths through the woods. He had taken MaryAnna there on a father-daughter date at the beginning of her fifth grade year. They had collected hazelnuts together. He walked down the same path they had chosen together that day, remembering how MaryAnna had boasted of gathering more nuts than he.

At the point of the path where a portion of an old stone wall lined the walk, he sat down. From where he sat, he could see the place where the path he was following split. He studied the fork in the path. He couldn't help but compare it to the choice he had ahead. One way seemed to have been cleared by a tractor. There were no brambles or large branches obstructing the view. He could see for almost a mile down it, and it was straight and even. The other way looked like it was not frequented much. Grass had been allowed to grow on it, and the underbrush was unchecked, making its way in from the edges. It was the kind of path for which he would want to make sure that he wore pants, he thought to himself as he looked at the thorns leaning inward on both sides.

There was no way for him to see where this path led from where he was seated. Closing his eyes, he prayed and asked God to confirm whether or not he was supposed to stay and continue this mission on his own, not knowing what the path would look like. He was tempted to move back to the States or to go and join the team in Rennes. Staying in Nantes with the three interns and no others on the leadership team felt daunting, scary and unpredictable, especially in light of what had just happened. On the other hand, he couldn't stand the thought of leaving the believers who were so faithful to meet together every week and needed a leader.

For a few moments, in his mind's eye, he was back at Harding University, sitting at the edge of the lily pool once again. The lights were blinking off and on. He remembered feeling so lost, so desperate, on that day long ago at the end of his senior year. He thought he had no direction for his future, and he was convinced he had ruined any chance of winning Marcie's heart.

It seemed to Jack that unseen forces were always barging in and interrupting his journey. He would begin on a certain trajectory, and inevitably something would stop him every time. He would come to a moment of crisis, wondering what to do next, and how to get back on the path. *But what,* he wondered, *if the source of the interruptions is the One I love most? What if it is God, trying to get my attention? Steering me in a different direction because of something specific and new that He has in mind? Maybe I have had a tendency to veer away from God's plan, and He has had to interrupt me to get me on the right path!*

*God, I need your help. Please pick up this ugly mess of shattered pieces and make something beautiful like only You can.*

God had not solved all of his problems that night at the edge of the pool with the blinking lights, but He did bring resolution over the course of time. Looking back, Jack could now see God's plan so clearly: He had wanted to work on Jack's heart first, before any other parts of the plan could be revealed. The words of Matthew 6:33 came to him. "But seek first his kingdom and his righteousness, and all these things shall be yours as well." He could see now that he had to give up the career he had hoped for as well as his hope of marriage. He had to put God first and give everything else up for the kingdom.

And then, just as God had sent the angel down to stop Abraham from sacrificing Isaac in Genesis, God did not require Jack to sacrifice his desires after all. The internship he'd sought came to him, and a few years later, he and Marcie were married. Together they had been able to pursue his vision of mission work in France. But first, he had to be willing to surrender all selfish ambition to God.

147

He put his head in his hands and ran his fingers through his hair, still chocolate-brown but now with a gray streak here and there. "Lord," he cried out, "I thought I knew the path I have been on was the right one. What would You have me do? I am willing to give up this dream of being in France as a missionary. And I am also willing to stay even if You would have me carry on alone. Give me a sign like You did for Gideon in the book of Judges with the fleece."

Right then he heard a scratching noise from behind a tree. He sat up abruptly and turned to see if a large animal had approached. Instead he saw the head of a gray squirrel poking out from a branch just behind his head. The squirrel stared at him so intently it was almost comical.

Jack smiled. He knew when God was trying to get his attention. As he watched, the squirrel scampered away, heading down the path lined with grass and brambles.

Peace as he had not felt for a long time washed over him as he drove back home. He thought again with fondness about his proposal to Marcie in the park in St. Louis, reading aloud to her Proverbs 30:18-19, "Three things are too wonderful for me; four I do not understand: the way of an eagle in the sky, the way of a serpent on a rock, the way of a ship on the high seas, and the way of a man with a maiden." He remembered as they walked together how they first noticed a large bird flying overhead that looked a lot like an eagle. And then a few steps later, they both saw a snake slithering quickly across the path in front of them. Just inside the park entrance, their eyes were drawn to small boys sailing toy boats on the lake. He remembered, as he stood there holding the hand of the woman of his dreams, how he'd thanked God for the clearest confirmation of His plan he had ever received in his life.

Many more clear signs from Him would follow: the Wilsons' joining them, the calling to Nantes through Serge, the success of the Colony Harmony French Christian church camp that he had cofounded, the growing of the church in Nantes, and even the episode of St. Louis friends helping his family through the airport. He saw clearly how God had been leading him steadily along.

Within the last twenty-four hours, he felt that God had granted him two potential signs to urge him to stay in Nantes with his family: the story of Lucy in *Prince Caspian* and the squirrel choosing the difficult path in the park. Curious, he decided to watch for a third sign as final confirmation. He pulled the van into the driveway and entered his home to the smell of *crêpes* and *galettes* cooking in the kitchen.

"Jack, I have something to tell you!" Marcie exclaimed.

She kissed her husband and then burst forth with her news. "I spoke with our neighbor Catherine. She is planning to come to the Tuesday night Bible study next week. I told her how embarrassed we were by some of the comments that were made at the first study she attended and that I was so thankful she wanted to come again after that meeting. Her response was priceless, Jack. She said, 'It is so sad that people wait until they are in such embarrassing conditions before they seek a relationship with Jesus.' Can you believe it?"

*Ha!* Jack thought. *Finally someone gets it!*

Before he could respond, Marcie continued. "I just checked the mail. There's a letter from Bordeaux. It looks like it's from Jerry Lee, one of the missionaries there."

Jack took the letter from Marcie's hands and sat down at the kitchen table to read it. The butter sizzled on the *crêpe* pan, and the batter sent out an aroma of sugar, eggs, and vanilla as it bubbled and cooked on the stovetop.

Dear Jack,

I have heard about what your team is going through in Nantes and I am praying for your family.

The church here in Bordeaux is doing well. My wife, Joy, and I have been here three years with the Ellises and the Shoulders. We have just learned that four interns are committing to minister with our church for an indefinite amount of time: three years or more.

I have a lot of respect for you and for your walk with the Lord. Joy and I feel compelled to help you in Nantes, if you will have us.

Will you pray about this as well? Perhaps soon we can talk on the phone. I would love to hear your thoughts.

I have no ambition but to do the will of the Father.

Sincerely,

Jerry

Jack folded the paper gently and replaced it in its envelope. He couldn't keep his lips from pursing into a smile. He reached up to wipe his eyes. So this was the third sign.

Marcie turned around. "Jack?" she asked with something like both concern and excitement in her voice. "Are you okay?"

"Yes," he said. "Oh, yes, I am."

He looked up toward heaven and then back at Marcie. "Why is it me that God has chosen to be a missionary in Nantes? I am just an ordinary guy. I'm nothing special. What exactly do you think God sees in me?"

"Oh Jack," Marcie answered, "don't you see? That is exactly why God has chosen you. God uses ordinary people to do extraordinary things. Yes, sometimes we think too highly of ourselves, and God humbles us again and again. But God has been and will always be the God who uses the plain and simple to do something great. That is when we can best see His glory."

"Marcie," Jack said with confidence, "I'm ready to be ordinary for Him."

"Me too," said Marcie.

# EPILOGUE

Buddy and Maurine Jones (portrayed as Jack and Marcie in this story) lived in Nantes, France, and served as missionaries there until Christmas of 1990. Buddy then became a preacher at University Church of Christ in Tuscaloosa, Alabama, until 2005. He and Maurine now live in Columbus, Georgia, where Buddy still preaches at Chattahoochee Valley Church every Sunday.

Since his return to the States, Buddy has spoken at Christian lectureships, given seminars, and preached in France, Switzerland, Kenya, Romania, Mauritius, and many cities across the southern United States. He is still open to God's call and stands at the ready. As veteran missionaries, Buddy and Maurine visit overseas missionaries every couple of years.

Maurine has followed Buddy back and forth across the Atlantic time after time, joining wholeheartedly in his calling. She has always had the heart of a missionary. Following her return to the States, she taught grade school in Tuscaloosa for a few years and then codirected the University Church Preschool until she and Buddy moved to Georgia. There she oversaw the work of teachers at St. Luke's Preschool. She now serves as a part-time secretary of the Chattahoochee Valley Church where Buddy preaches.

Now that their children are gown, Maurine enjoys ministering alongside Buddy with Bible studies, helping the poor, teaching Sunday school and ladies' classes, and mentoring young women. She is also an advocate for the orphans of the Ring Road day school in Kisumu, Kenya, where Sarah (portrayed as baby Caroline Ruth) now serves alongside her husband and three children. Maurine enjoys visiting her children and grandchildren, to whom her heart is still drawn.

The *Église du Christ de Nantes* is no more. The Christians remaining in the city who were once members struggle to hold on to their faith. They love receiving occasional visits from Buddy and Maurine. The future of the church in their city is yet to be revealed. As a nation, France is becoming more and more of a racial melting pot. Will this phenomenon push the French people toward or away from God? On the surface, things change, but the fact that mankind everywhere needs Jesus remains the same.

Buddy and Maurine served faithfully in their time. Who will help the people of France see the answers to their pain now and in the future?

Are you ordinary? Do you feel like a "plain old" fill-in-the-blank with your occupation or identity person? John 4:35 says, "I tell you, open your eyes and look at the fields! They are ripe for harvest" (NIV). Jesus shares these words with His disciples after a plain, old, ordinary, and worn out woman leaves her water jar at the well because God reaches into the muck and mire of her life through Jesus to make something beautiful and new. Once the talk of the town for her sin, she becomes God's extraordinary messenger to the people where she lives.

There is a reason that the church in Nantes, France, is no more. If God allowed Joseph to be sold into slavery and alienated from his family, if God allowed His own son to die, if He allowed the earth to be flooded, and if He allowed the Israelites to wander in the desert for forty years and Peter to be put in prison and Steven to be stoned and John to be exiled and Paul to be shipwrecked, then there is nothing so bad or so hopeless in anyone's life that can't be redeemed by God the Father. He is the One who restored Joseph to his family, raised Jesus from the dead, repopulated the earth after His promise never to flood it again, brought the Israelites into the Promised Land, sent the angel to deliver Peter, appeared to Steven as he was dying, revealed Himself to John in exile, and rescued every sailor on Paul's ship when it was wrecked.

So what about us?

Wait and see. Get ready. If you are ordinary, then God is calling you and me. Listen to Him. We have a journey ahead of us. It's time for Him to make our journey an extraordinary one.

# ABOUT THE AUTHOR

Anna Caulley writes out of her passion for words, for Jesus, and for words about Jesus. Her entire life has been centered on the church, its ministries, and mission efforts in the States and overseas. Her husband, father, grandfather, five uncles, three cousins, and two brothers-in-law are ministers. She and her husband have been part of a church plant in Colorado. Two of her roommates from college are foreign missionaries.

Anna is a French teacher living in Perry, Georgia, with her husband, Don, and three sons. She is a 1998 graduate of Harding University with a degree in French and Education. This writing is her first novel.

As a teacher of Ladies' Bible classes, adult Sunday school classes, and children's classes as well as serving as a children's ministry leader, Anna has learned many valuable life lessons. She loves having heart-to-heart conversations with people, going for walks, "dating" her husband, singing at church, teaching Vacation Bible School, listening to her oldest son play the guitar, and being a soccer mom.